"We'll have to postpone the wedding."

Luke's voice sounded apologetic.

This was it, then. The final proof of what Vanessa had told her. Sue sat down. Her limbs felt heavy. "I think," she said slowly, "that we'd better postpone it for good."

His head jerked up. "What the hell are you talking about?"

She licked her dry lips. "I've had time to think since I've been on my own these few days. Well—just for a time, after we...after—" her voice faltered "—after we made love, you persuaded me that it would work. But it wouldn't. We scarcely know each other. We've both admitted we're not in love, so what have we got?"

His gray eyes were fixed on her, but she couldn't tell what he was thinking. "I'd have thought it was obvious what we've got," he said.

"You mean—sex?"

Books by Marjorie Lewty

HARLEQUIN ROMANCE

HARLEQUIN PRESENTS

These books may be available at your local bookseller.

Don't miss any of our special offers. Write to us at the following address for information on our newest releases.

Harlequin Reader Service
P.O. Box 52040, Phoenix, AZ 85072-2040
Canadian address: P.O. Box 2800, Postal Station A,
5170 Yonge St., Willowdale, Ont. M2N 6J3

A Lake in Kyoto

Marjorie Lewty

Harlequin Books

TORONTO • NEW YORK • LONDON
AMSTERDAM • PARIS • SYDNEY • HAMBURG
STOCKHOLM • ATHENS • TOKYO • MILAN

Original hardcover edition published in 1985
by Mills & Boon Limited

ISBN 0-373-02746-X

Harlequin Romance first edition February 1986

Copyright © 1985 by Marjorie Lewty.
Philippine copyright 1985. Australian copyright 1985.

All rights reserved. Except for use in any review, the reproduction or utilization
of this work in whole or in part in any form by any electronic, mechanical or
other means, now known or hereafter invented, including xerography,
photocopying and recording, or in any information storage or retrieval system,
is forbidden without the permission of the publisher, Harlequin Enterprises
Limited, 225 Duncan Mill Road, Don Mills, Ontario, Canada M3B 3K9. All the
characters in this book have no existence outside the imagination of the
author and have no relation whatsoever to anyone bearing the same name
or names. They are not even distantly inspired by any individual known
or unknown to the author, and all the incidents are pure invention.

The Harlequin trademarks, consisting of the words HARLEQUIN ROMANCE
and the portrayal of a Harlequin, are trademarks of Harlequin Enterprises
Limited; the portrayal of a Harlequin is registered in the United States Patent
and Trademark Office and in the Canada Trade Marks Office.

Printed in U.S.A.

CHAPTER ONE

SHE was here. She was really in Japan. And best of all any moment now she would see Steve again after four whole years. Sue could hardly breathe for excitement as she stood beside her hand-baggage in the busy concourse of Tokyo Airport, a tallish, slender girl with pale-gold hair, streaked almost to white by the Australian sun, and a humorous tilt to her lips. Her dark blue eyes sparkled with happy anticipation, but truth to tell the butterflies in her tummy seemed to be multiplying by the second as she searched the moving mass of faces around—mostly ivory-skinned Japanese faces—without finding the thin, rather serious English face of her brother Steve.

She looked at her watch. She'd altered it when instructed on the flight from Sydney, but it had been playing up for weeks now and she was sure that it was showing the wrong time. At a guess she reckoned that she must have been standing here for quite twenty minutes. Steve had always been reasonably punctual. Surely he should have been here by now? He wouldn't leave her stranded alone in a foreign airport where the notices were all in Japanese script and the tannoy kept on twittering out words that were bewilderingly incomprehensible.

Sue moved restlessly as the minutes passed, her eyes darting around the huge, noisy, busy concourse. What if she was waiting in the wrong place? On the 'phone Steve had said 'I'll meet you at the airport'. That had seemed definite enough at the time but now it began to seem horribly vague. What if there was another airport in Tokyo? What if he'd seen her from the

distance and not recognized her and gone away again?
Four years of life in the wide open spaces of an
Australian cattle station had probably changed her
more than she realized. Sixteen-and-a-half to nearly
twenty-one makes a difference to a girl. 'Steve won't
know you—you've filled out so nicely,' Aunt Meg had
said with some pride when Sue had left the homestead
at the crack of dawn yesterday morning to fly to
Sydney with Ross on the first leg of the journey to
Tokyo.

Ross! Just for a moment, standing alone among the
passing crowd of strangers, she wished that he was still
beside her. Ross—burly, slow-speaking, unflappable,
reliable. Then she thought—*No*. Wasn't Ross just one
of the 'dear octopus' tentacles that were spreading out
from the homestead in Langaroo? One of the ties of
affection and gratitude that were binding her more and
more closely to the prospect of a life that sometimes
seemed as flat and empty as the wide dusty acres of the
cattle station itself? A prospect that often filled her
with dismay.

She wriggled her slim shoulders as if she could push
away the problems that had been nagging at her
recently. These few days in Japan would give her time
to sort things out. And she'd banked on explaining the
difficulties to Steve and hoped that he might suggest some
solution.

But where *was* Steve? She was beginning to feel
definitely uneasy now. All the other passengers from
her flight had dispersed and it seemed silly to go on
waiting. She mustn't panic, she told herself. Somehow
she and Steve had missed each other, but she knew the
address of his apartment in Tokyo, she'd just have to
find out how to get herself there.

An enquiries desk, that was what she needed. There
was a row of desks along one side of the big hall.

Would they understand English there if she joined one of the queues and would she understand their instructions? She'd just have to chance it and hope for the best.

It was then that she noticed that the tall dark man who stood beside a pillar a few yards away, frowning and consulting his watch, was still there. She'd noticed him before, he was the kind of man who stands out in a crowd. Head and shoulders taller than anyone around, wearing a grey suit that sat immaculately over broad shoulders, he was conspicuous among the shorter Japanese men, so correctly dressed in their dark business suits, and the hot, weary-looking tourists humping their baggage or pushing their trolleys.

Sue got a strong impression that he was British, she didn't quite know why. Perhaps it was his air of detachment, the way his eyes moved over the crowd around, that touch of arrogance that didn't go down at all well in Langeroo. Four years of living and working among the men at the cattle station had left Sue in no doubt that her adolescent dreams of a tall, dark glamorous story-book hero for a lover were best forgotten. In Langeroo you kept quiet about the books you read, the music you loved, the places you yearned for. The talk was all of cattle and sheep and droughts and market prices.

Sue hesitated, suddenly a little uncertain of speaking to a total stranger. But the man looked at home here, he was the much-travelled, cosmopolitan type who could almost certainly give her the information she wanted. It was worth risking.

She picked up her heavy hand-baggage, hitched her shoulder bag more firmly and marched up to him with more confidence than she felt.

'Hello—do you speak English by any chance?' she said. Four years ago, fresh from England, she might have begun with a tentative '. . . er—excuse me . . .' but life in Australia had pared away most of her natural shyness—made her more forthcoming. She smiled up at the tall man hopefully, quite unconscious of the picture she made in her inexpensive blue suit, a shade darker than her eyes, her luxurious ash-blonde hair framing her eager face.

A pair of steel-grey eyes narrowed under thick dark brows as the man glanced down at her. There was a moment of complete silence and Sue thought she had made a mistake after all, that he didn't understand what she said. Then his face went chillingly blank, as if a shutter had closed over it. He made a dismissive gesture with one hand. 'Nothing doing,' he said. 'Get lost, will you?'

Sue stared up at him, totally bewildered, her lips parted in amazement. What had she done or said, for goodness sake, to invite a reply like that? Then, suddenly, as she stared at that hard, closed face, the penny dropped. Goodness, she thought, he imagines I'm trying to—to—what was the word?—to solicit him.

Restraining a chuckle with an effort she said, 'Don't be alarmed, I have no ulterior motive. I merely thought you might be English and I wondered if you would tell me the best way of getting to my brother's apartment in Tokyo. He should have been here to meet me but he hasn't arrived and I want to——'

'Hold on a minute.' The hard, shuttered expression had changed to a frown. 'What's your brother's name?'

She didn't like his tone and if she hadn't dumped her heavy bag at her feet she would have walked away quickly. 'I don't think that is any concern of yours,' she said loftily. 'I merely asked for information.'

He gave a weary, exasperated sigh, indicating

plainly that she was a dim-witted female who was wasting his valuable time. 'Is your brother's name Larkin? Steve Larkin?'

She nodded speechlessly, apprehension trickling through her. Where was Steve and who was this insolent stranger?

'And your name is . . .?'

'Sue Larkin.' She lifted her chin a fraction. 'And now you've identified me, I hope, as not being a—a streetwalker with dark designs on you, perhaps you'll tell me what all this is about?'

His harsh features relaxed but his smile didn't reach his eyes. 'I'm Luke Masters. Your brother asked me to meet you but I'm afraid I didn't recognise you from his description.'

'But why isn't Steve here himself? Is he all right? Has anything happened to him?' She was suddenly cold and hollow inside. Hardly knowing what she was doing she grasped his arm and shook it impetuously.

He covered her hand with his to stop her and a strange, unfamiliar sensation gripped her inside. If she had stopped to analyse it she would have put it down to fear about Steve. 'Don't panic, it's nothing too bad,' he said rather curtly. 'He was in a road accident yesterday evening, in Kyoto. He's in hospital there.'

Sue was afraid she was going to pass out. She swayed on her feet. 'Oh please—tell me quickly—how bad is it? He's not . . .?'

'Calm down,' he said and his hand still covered hers. He glanced around, no doubt fearing that she was going to make a scene. 'I told you—nothing too bad. A broken arm and various nasty bruises. He'll have to stay in hospital for a few days, that's all.'

'Oh,' said Sue weakly, and then, even more faintly, 'Do you think I could—could sit down somewhere, please. Just for a few minutes.'

'Of course.' He looked at her white face, then he picked up her heavy travelling bag in one hand, while he put his other arm round her and led the way across the concourse into a coffee-bar.

'Sit here,' he said. 'I'll get you a drink.'

Sue closed her eyes because everything was revolving round her in a most curious way but in a very short time she felt a touch on her shoulder and saw that the man had come back and put a mug of black coffee in front of her on the table. The bar was crowded and he stood behind her while she drank the coffee. After she had drained the mug the room stopped revolving. She looked up at him. 'Thank you, that was very nice,' she said politely.

'If you're OK we'll make a move, then.' He gripped her elbow and led her through the bewildering complex of the airport terminal and into a taxi.

'Where are we going?' Sue asked.

'My hotel,' Luke Masters said. 'We'll go on to Kyoto tomorrow.'

'*Tomorrow?*' Sue's voice went up a couple of tones. 'Can't I see Steve today?'

'No,' said Luke Masters. 'You can't. Kyoto is over three hundred miles away. It's much too late to get there today.'

'Oh.' Sue sat staring out of the taxi window. It was too dark to see anything much outside and she was gripped by a terrible sense of desolation. If only Steve were sitting beside her instead of this impersonal stranger who made her feel as if she were being a nuisance.

She had dreamed of nothing but this trip for weeks, ever since Steve had written to tell her that he was marrying his Japanese girl-friend, Mariko, and that Sue *must* come to Japan for the wedding. 'It's time we got together again, little sister,' he'd written. 'It's been far too long. But now I seem to be making my way in the firm and I'm sending on the money for your fare. You must come a day or two before the wedding and then there'll be time to meet Mariko's family in Kyoto and see some of the local sights. Lots of temples and gardens and things that will appeal to my artistic little Sue, no doubt. You'll be able to do plenty of sketching.'

Sketching! Sue had smiled at that. Steve evidently imagined that life on a cattle station had left her exactly the same as when they had said goodbye at Heathrow nearly four years ago—he to go off to his promising new job in Japan, she to make a new home for herself with her unknown aunt and uncle in Australia. She could still remember the black misery of that moment.

But the misery was over now, although the longing for England, for the lakes and mountains that had been her childhood delight, had never gone away altogether. Sometimes she would forget for weeks at a time, and then some little thing would remind her and she would be pierced through and through with a sharp pain like hunger.

She was aware that the man beside her had spoken and she turned her head towards the shadowy figure in the opposite corner of the seat. 'I'm sorry?' she said vaguely.

'I said, did you have a good journey?' He didn't even try to suppress a yawn.

'Yes, thank you,' Sue said stiffly. 'It was good of you to meet me.' She would have liked to add that he needn't bother any further with her when he was so obviously bored to death with the assignment, but an independent spirit can only take one so far and the plain fact was that she needed his help in this strange country.

'It was the least I could do,' he said, 'in the circumstances.'

When he didn't appear to be going to enlarge on that statement she asked, 'What circumstances would those be?'

'Your brother and I had been out to dinner together and we were both involved in the accident,' he said matter-of-factly.

'Oh goodness—but what about you? You weren't hurt?' Sue said quickly, her voice suddenly warm and concerned.

He laughed drily. 'They didn't seem anxious to keep me in hospital at any rate.'

'Then you *were* hurt?' Sue insisted. 'And you came all the way to Tokyo to meet me. Oh, you shouldn't have done, you really shouldn't.' Suddenly she was getting a new angle on this man. You must never judge by appearances, she scolded herself. He was probably feeling rotten still, maybe in pain.

'Don't fuss, there's a good girl,' he said briefly. 'I'm OK.' He leaned his head back against the seat and she could see that his eyes were closed.

Don't fuss, he'd said, and the words stirred a memory. That was what Daddy had said when she tried to stop him going out with the mountain rescue team on that awful winter night four years ago, when he had a bad cold already. 'Don't fuss, sweetheart,' he'd said. 'Of course I must go.'

Perhaps if she'd fussed hard enough then she might have stopped him, she just *might*. And then he might not have got pleurisy and he might still be alive now, and she might be living happily with him in her beloved Lake District. So many 'mights', and it was no good dwelling on the past, you had to deal with the present, and the present was that Steve was lying in hospital, miles away, and she had to rely on this difficult, moody stranger to get her to him, so she'd better make the best of it.

She was silent for the rest of the drive, which seemed to take a long time. The traffic became more and more dense and then they were in the city and the taxi had come to a halt in a traffic jam.

Sue stared out of the window. The wide street was as light as day, sparkling with coloured flashing neon lights. Long illuminated banner-like signs in all sizes hung overhead, decorated with their strange Japanese characters that she wished she could read. There was even one sign that she *could* read—it said 'Pants Shop'. She couldn't help a giggle as she saw that.

The man beside her gave a start and said, 'Good lord, we're here, that was quick,' and she knew he'd been asleep.

'What a fantastic place,' Sue said.

Luke Masters glanced briefly out of the window at the glittering street. 'Commercial,' he said in a dismissive tone.

'I suppose so,' Sue sighed. 'But it's rather lovely all the same. Look at that sign—the colours—that cerulean blue with the vermilion.'

He turned his head and she thought that for the first time she had said something that caught his attention. 'The Japanese are incapable of making anything ugly,' he said. 'You'll find that out as you go around here. Beauty and harmony are still vitally important to them.' It was the longest speech he had made since they met.

The taxi started with a jerk and began to weave its way perilously through the mass of traffic and finally pulled in before a giant hotel building.

Luke Masters seemed to have everything under control and very soon they were escorted up in a lift by a uniformed Japanese girl who unlocked a door in a long, carpeted corridor and stood aside to usher Sue in, bowing and smiling all the time and trusting, in good English, that Sue's stay would be comfortable.

Sue bowed and smiled back because that seemed the polite thing to do and said that she was sure it would be, and indeed the room was luxury itself after her small white bedroom at the homestead. It wasn't quite what she'd expected in Japan. From the books she had read she had pictured cool empty rooms, their floor covered with *tatami* mats, divided from other rooms by sliding screens with translucent paper panels. But this room was just like any other bedroom, although very much larger and grander than any bedroom that Sue had seen. But then, she had never stayed in a luxury hotel in her life.

She heard the door close behind the Japanese girl and looked round for Luke, who was standing just inside the door. She gave him an uncertain little smile. 'Thank you, I'll be quite OK here now,' she said. She'd feel more comfortable when she was alone. The man made her jittery.

He didn't reply and she saw that his face was chalky under its tan as he stared at her dazedly. Then he swayed on his feet, groping for support and finding none. Sue flew across the room and grabbed his hand tightly. 'Hang on to me,' she said and thrust an arm round his waist under his light jacket. His body felt hard and unyielding and for a moment she thought his weight was going to topple them both on to the floor but somehow she managed to steady him and together they staggered across the room and they both collapsed on to the wide bed. Sue was gasping for breath and she felt the weight of his body half across hers. It was a most peculiar sensation and for a moment she had a feeling of closeness, almost of intimacy, that made her heart beat unsteadily before she wriggled away and stood up.

He opened his eyes and frowned dazedly up at her. Then he moistened his lips. 'What . . .' he mumbled, trying to lift himself on one elbow.

'Don't try and get up for a bit,' Sue told him, pushing him down again gently by the shoulders. He lay back against the pillows, grimacing, his eyelids drooping. Within moments he heaved a deep sigh and she saw that he was asleep.

'Well!' breathed Sue. This was a very strange experience indeed. What did she do next? Wake him up? But she couldn't do that, he looked absolutely dead to the world. She stood beside the bed looking down at him, seeing the lines of exhaustion smooth themselves out as he sank deeper and deeper into sleep. Relaxed, his face had changed, looked younger, happier, with the defencelessness that sleep brings. Impossible, almost, to remember that hard, shuttered look that he had turned on her at the airport.

He really was very good-looking—a strong face certainly; that showed in the dominant nose and square chin, which had the faintest of clefts in it. His hair was dark, with the gloss that comes from perfect health. It was swept across his wide brow and a thick lock had fallen forward over one eye. She reached down carefully and smoothed it back as she would have done for Brian, her young cousin at the homestead, and oddly, as she did so, she was conscious of the same little rush of tenderness that she sometimes felt for Brian when he was asleep.

She wondered how old this man Luke was—a good deal older than Steve certainly. He'd be in his middle thirties, to Steve's twenty-seven. Was he a member of Steve's company? she wondered. Steve's job was in the office of a big, international concern with a branch in Tokyo which dealt with its textile side. Oh well, she'd probably find out about Luke Masters all in good time. Meanwhile she'd just have to decide what to do next.

She realised suddenly that she was very hungry indeed. She had been too excited to eat much on the plane, and her last meal had been early this morning— breakfast at the home of Ross's uncle in Sydney, where they had stayed the night. She prowled round the bedroom, looking at the push-buttons with their identities marked in about six different languages. She just hadn't the nerve to push any of them, or to try the telephone beside the bed. The wall-fitment included a little fridge furnished with several mini-bottles of drinks. She opened one labelled lemonade and rummaged in her travelling bag for the remainder of the packet of sandwiches that Auntie Meg had insisted on providing for the journey. That had been yesterday morning and they had aged considerably since then; the edges of the bread were curled up and the cheese was hard, but when she had munched her way through the lot and drunk the lemonade she felt better.

She sat back in the cushioned chair and surveyed the sleeping man on the bed. Nothing in her life had prepared her to deal with a situation like this. She supposed she could try to wake him up—give him a good shake and push him off to his own room. But he was sleeping so deeply and peacefully now, breathing regularly. He really did seem absolutely fagged out and she didn't have the heart to disturb him. Added to which there was always the possibility that he had done some damage to himself in the accident; if that was so she wouldn't want to risk making it worse. Sleep is the best doctor of all, Auntie Meg always said, and Auntie Meg was usually right about such things.

She consulted her watch again but now it had stopped. It would help to know the time—give her something to hang on to in this very odd situation. She went across to the bed and looked down at Luke Masters. He had sunk into a very deep sleep now, she doubted if she could wake him if she tried. He was lying on his right side and she saw the edge of a wristwatch peeping out from under the shirt cuff on his left arm, which was thrown across the pillow beside his head. Gingerly she pushed back the cuff and exposed a slim, expensive-looking watch to view. Oddly enough, although Sue's intention had been to see the time, she found herself staring at the strong bony wrist with the dark, fine hairs round the gold watch-bracelet before she pulled herself together and consulted the hands of the watch, which told her that it was twenty minutes to eleven.

Well past my bedtime, she told herself, trying to see the funny side of all this. She usually went to bed quite early back at the homestead and read herself to sleep. There wasn't much else to do in the evenings unless you were hooked on television, which she wasn't. But a book was a different matter. Sue loved books—all kinds of books and she had always read everything she could get her hands on.

When she was young, back home in the English Lake District, the cottage had groaned with her father's books. They had spilled over tables, fallen from shelves, covered walls; even the stairwell had been lined with books. When the cottage was sold, with all the furniture, the new owners had looked doubtfully at the books, and Steve had had the job of getting a secondhand dealer from Kendal to take them away. Sue had disappeared up into the fells on the day the dealer collected the books and come back hours later, white-faced and puffy-eyed. With the cottage

denuded of books she had to accept at last the truth
that her father was dead, that she would never see him
again. That was the night she told Steve that she
would go to Australia to Auntie Meg and Uncle Ray,
who had written to offer her a home.

'Are you sure?' Steve had asked, in his serious,
concerned way. 'Will you be OK there? I don't really
like the idea of us splitting up now. I wish I could take
you to Japan with me, but that's out of the question. I
could turn down the offer of the job, I suppose . . .'

He would have done too, if Sue had asked him to.
At twenty-three Steve had suddenly become the man
of the family and he took his responsibilities seriously.
But this new job that he had just landed in Japan was
so exactly what he wanted—he'd been over the moon
when the offer came. 'Of course you can't turn it
down, don't be crazy,' Sue told him. 'I'll be perfectly
OK. I've always wanted to see the world.'

'I wouldn't call a homestead in Queensland exactly
seeing the world,' Steve said doubtfully. 'And what
about your art course?' Sue had finished school and
had just started an art course in Lancaster, at the
college where their father had taught part-time.

'I expect I'll find something of the sort out there,'
she said vaguely. 'Anyway, I shouldn't think I've
much chance of getting into the Tate Gallery.' Art
didn't seem to matter very much now. Truth to tell,
nothing mattered very much when Daddy wasn't here
to share it with her.

'Well if you're sure . . .' Steve said at last and she
saw that he was trying hard not to show his relief.

'I'm sure,' Sue said, and three weeks later she had
flown off to Australia.

Four years ago. Four years since she had seen Steve
because somehow he had never got around to visiting.
At first he was too busy learning the language and his

new job. '. . . and saving hard to get a bit of capital behind us. When I've saved up enough perhaps you might join me in Japan,' he had told her in one of his letters, which had tended to arrive less frequently as the time went by. And then he had met Mariko and fallen in love, and after that there wasn't any talk of Sue joining him in Japan.

Not until the wedding. And what *about* the wedding? Sue worried, sitting here in a Tokyo hotel bedroom, with a strange man asleep on the bed and Steve lying in a hospital miles away. Was there going to be a wedding? Friday was only five days off; would Steve be sufficiently recovered in time? She suddenly felt dispirited and weary. The man Luke looked as if he would sleep for hours. On *her* bed, too, she reminded herself. She supposed she could find out the number of his room and try to explain to the reception clerk what had happened, so that she could change rooms and have a bed to sleep on, but that seemed so complicated.

OK, Mr Luke Masters, she thought, I'll just have to let you share my bed. I'm certainly not going to sit in a chair all night. Suddenly the funny side struck her. If he wakened up and found her on the other side of the bed he *would* think the worst, the suspicious brute.

Chuckling a little hysterically Sue removed her jacket and skirt and blouse and hung them over the back of a chair. On the bottom of the bed was spread a white cotton garment—a kimono, she supposed. This was obviously supplied by the hotel for her use and she stuck her arms into the wide sleeves and pulled it round her. Taking her toilet things from her bag, she opened a door on the far side of the room and found a small, luxury bathroom. She was much too tired to have a bath, that could wait until the morning, but it would be nice to be able to wash her face and brush her teeth.

Five minutes later she returned to the bedroom. The man on the bed hadn't moved. He was so still that Sue felt a sudden stab of fear. She leaned over the bed, her eyes searching his face anxiously. Then she felt the warmth of his breath on her cheek and sighed with relief. For a moment she stood there, her face only inches from his, and again that strange new sensation gripped her inside. She straightened quickly, breathing rather fast. This, she supposed, was the sexual thing you read so much about in books, but which she had never experienced before, and been inclined to think was probably much exaggerated. The kisses she had received at the monthly 'hops' from hopeful young men who worked at the homestead had certainly never made her feel like this, and Auntie Meg had made sure that kisses were as far as it went. Auntie Meg had strong views about the conduct suitable for a young lady and the permissive society was something that existed in the big bad cities like New York, London and Sydney, possibly, but certainly not in Langeroo.

What, wondered Sue, would Auntie Meg have advised her to do in this situation? Scream for help, probably, she thought, with a small affectionate grin. Instead, she carefully unfastened the laces of Luke Masters's elegant black shoes and pulled them off one by one, laying them carefully beside the bed. He had collapsed on top of the bed covers and she couldn't lift him to cover him up. She went through all the drawers in the room and found a couple of fleecy pink blankets on the shelf above the hanging rail in the wardrobe. Pulling down the largest and softest one she laid it over the sleeping man. Then, hardly daring to breathe, she crept round to the other side of the bed and climbed stealthily on to it, easing herself under the blanket, letting her head drop wearily on to the smooth pillow.

Ah ... heaven! Sue drew in a long comfortable weary sigh. It had been quite a day. But tomorrow would be better because tomorrow she would see Steve and then she would know the score and not be dependent on this formidable individual on the other side of the bed. Sleep—lovely! She closed her eyes.

Then she froze as the bed seemed to rock under her. An earthquake? she thought, panicking. She had read that they had earthquakes in Japan. But no, it was merely that the man beside her had heaved himself over on his other side. Beneath the blanket an arm was flung out and landed across her body, pressing heavily down on her ribs. 'Sweetheart—my lovely wife——' came a deep rumble of a voice from the depths of sleep, and then muttered words that sounded like, 'Darling Val——' Or was it 'Van', the muttered name? Sue found herself being drawn closer against the man's relaxed body; the warmth of it reached her through his light jacket, and her cotton kimono. She lay very still, her heart thumping painfully, shocked by the strength of the impulse that urged her to turn over to face him, to wind her arms round him. Was he going to wake up, she wondered in sudden panic. She *must* be up and about before he wakened, it would be too embarrassing if he found her sharing the bed with him and difficult to explain. But he didn't waken and by and by Sue relaxed.

It was so warm and comfortable; she would just allow herself to sleep for a little while; then she would get up and wake him and he could go off to his own room when he'd taken the first edge off his fatigue. Gently she eased herself from under his arm, and to her surprise she felt suddenly lost and lonely. But of course it wouldn't do to stay like that—it wouldn't do at all. Sue yawned and closed her eyes again. Just a couple of hours, she thought ... Just a couple—of hours ...

Someone was shaking her arm and she wakened with a start to find the sun streaming into the room and a large figure looming above her. She blinked twice and was wide awake and it was Luke Masters standing beside the bed frowning down at her with anger written all over his dark, somewhat dishevelled-looking face. 'What was the idea of us sharing a bed?' he snarled, indicating the half of the bed on which he had spent the night. 'Why the hell couldn't you have wakened me up so that I could have gone to my own room?'

So much for being thoughtful for his welfare! Sue slid off the bed and pulled herself up to her full height, turning a clear blue stare on him. 'Because you were so fast asleep that it would have taken an earthquake to waken you. And anyway you flaked out before you went to sleep and I thought maybe you might have been more hurt in the accident than you let on. It seemed to me wiser to let you sleep,' she added with some dignity.

'Oh,' he grunted ungraciously. He went over to the mirror and stroked his unshaven chin.

Sue watched him. 'You're not still suspecting that I have designs on your—er—virtue, surely?' she said, keeping a straight face with an effort.

He continued to survey himself in the mirror for a few more seconds, raking back his dark hair. Then he turned and Sue saw faint amusement lurking behind the steel-grey depths of his eyes. 'The way I look at this moment I should think it highly unlikely any girl would fancy me,' he grinned.

But I would, Sue thought, shocked by the sudden certainty. She laughed to cover her confusion. 'You do look rather a desperado,' she said.

He came back and sat on the edge of the bed. 'You're a funny kid, little Sue,' he said. 'I haven't met a girl quite like you before.'

'Kid!' she came back at him indignantly. 'I'm nearly twenty-one.'

'A great age,' he agreed, his mouth twisting. 'You must have led a very full life.'

Sue's small face clouded and she shook her head rather despondently. 'That's just what I haven't done. Life on a farm in Australia, ten miles from the nearest neighbour, isn't what you call full. But I've read a lot,' she added, cheering up.

She saw that he was laughing at her. 'Very laudable, but no substitute for the real thing. We'll have to give you some experience of the great big world of men and women, then you can compare it with what happens in your books. And—even with the kindest and most innocent of intentions—you'll think twice before you kip down on a bed alongside a healthy male again.'

And a married male too, she thought, feeling a trifle guilty.

He was coming nearer to her as he spoke and now he was close in front of her, so close that she had either to stand with her body touching his, or sink backwards on to the bed. She did the latter and he promptly joined her there. 'Shaved or not,' he murmured, 'we could make a beginning with your education.'

She found herself pressed back and her mouth covered by his, and sanity faltered. His lips were firm and searching and the rough, scratchy hair on his chin sent trickles of excitement up and down her spine. His mouth moved teasingly, invitingly on hers and she found herself responding intuitively, her body growing warm and languorous in his arms as they closed round her under the cotton kimono. His kisses grew deeper, more urgent, and Sue's head whirled with the sudden ecstasy of the sensations he was arousing in her.

Then, suddenly, it was over. He released her and stood up. 'Lesson one,' he said and his voice was perfectly steady. 'You're a quick learner, young Sue. Or else . . .' his eyes narrowed '. . . life on the farm wasn't quite as cloistered as you choose to make out.'

She scrambled to her feet beside him, her eyes blazing blue fire. 'You can believe what you like, Mr Suspicious,' she shot at him. 'I don't tell lies.'

He smiled a cynical smile. 'Ever since Eve women have been telling lies to men. You won't convince me that you're the exception.'

'I don't want to convince you of anything,' she said. And then she had a sudden brainwave and added, 'What I want most at the moment is some breakfast.' That would show him that she hadn't been any more disturbed by his sudden onslaught than he had been himself. It didn't occur to her that she was contradicting what she had just said about telling lies.

She thought that he looked a trifle taken aback but he only said, 'Have you ordered breakfast then? While I was sleeping the sleep of the—er—just, did you fill in your little card?'

'What little card?'

He walked across to the door and Sue noticed for the first time that there was a card attached to the handle. He pulled it off and waved it in front of her eyes. 'You fill in your order before you go to bed and hang the card outside the door,' he said. 'Your breakfast is served in your room at the time you specify. That's the usual drill in hotels like this.'

Sue lifted her small chin. 'Oh, is it? Well, you can't expect me to know things like that, coming straight from the wilds of the outback, can you? I'm sure you'll be able to fix something.' She picked up her blouse and skirt from the back of the chair and turned to the bathroom. 'I'm going to have a shower. Will someone bring my breakfast up, then? I'm awfully hungry,' she added a trifle wistfully.

'Someone will,' he promised. 'I shall retire to my own room to repair the damage, and then I'll join you here to eat.'

He didn't ask for her agreement, he simply stated the fact. But Sue wasn't accustomed to men consulting her wishes—it wasn't really part of the Australian scene. Men made the decisions and by and large women fell in with them. So she just shrugged and went into the bathroom.

She took her time over her shower and the cool, refreshing water helped to calm down her racing thoughts. She still felt shaken by the impact of Luke Masters's personality but she certainly mustn't allow herself to be overwhelmed by it. It had been her first taste of real lovemaking, and, brief though it had been it had shown her that there were great yawning gaps in her experience of the man woman encounter. It would be the height of folly to imagine herself in love with the first man who disturbed her, and an older, experienced, married man at that. That would be the reaction of a sixteen-year-old and if she had been able to go on with art school she would have doubtless gone through that stage and out at the other side by now.

On the other hand it would be foolish to ignore Luke's undoubted charisma. Any girl would be impressed by him—and no doubt many had been. She tried to imagine what his wife was like. Very beautiful and very sophisticated no doubt. The idea gave her a small, unpleasant pang, which she quickly assured herself was ridiculous. She really must not let this man loom so large in her present situation; it was just the odd way that everything had happened and once they got to Kyoto she would probably not meet him again.

The thought of Kyoto set her worrying about Steve and wondering how he was and there wasn't room in her mind for anything else as she dressed and attended to the rest of her toilet. When she emerged, her cheeks glowing, her ash-blonde hair brushed to a satin sheen, and her neat blue skirt and white blouse flattering her slim figure, she felt ready to deal with the enigmatic Luke Masters and give as good as she got. Or if she couldn't risk clashing with him, at least she could make sure that he didn't overwhelm her.

In this Sue was, perhaps, a little too optimistic.

CHAPTER TWO

Sue emerged from the bathroom at exactly the same moment that Luke opened the door of the bedroom. She smiled at him a little tentatively. He had shaved, and groomed his dark hair, and changed into black jeans and a white open-neck shirt and he looked so shatteringly large and male and attractive that Sue felt suddenly shy when she remembered that only a few minutes ago he had held her in his arms and kissed her.

But if she felt awkward he certainly didn't. 'Ah, food!' He rubbed his hands together, striding across to the small table set in the window. 'You hungry? I know I am.'

He pulled out a chair for her and she sank into it. 'Coffee,' he mused, his eyes searching the table. 'Fruit juice—breads—muffins—preserves—pastries ... I didn't order anything cooked. This OK for you?'

'Oh *yes*, it looks wonderful. I'm ravenous,' Sue admitted, suddenly losing her shyness at the sight of such delicious food.

'Me too,' said Luke. 'Let's eat.' He tossed down a glass of orange juice and Sue followed suit and then they started on the main part of the meal. A quarter of an hour later the table was almost empty of food.'

Luke sat back in his chair. 'Now,' he said. 'Fire away.'

Sue's blue eyes opened wide and he added, 'You're dying to ask me questions, aren't you?'

'Well, yes I am,' she admitted. 'I want to know about Steve—and the wedding—and everything. And

27

perhaps about you, too, if you care to tell me,' she added with a little apologetic smile. 'I mean, have you known Steve long? I don't remember his mentioning your name in his letters. Although he hasn't written very often recently,' she added candidly.

'Too busy falling in love, no doubt.' The man's mouth took a downward tilt and there was acid in his tone. The remark wasn't intended to be a joke, and Sue ignored it.

There was a short silence before Luke spoke again. 'Steve and I are colleagues—we work for the same concern but I'm the new boy. I've only recently moved to his section and this is my first visit to Japan on company business—though I've been here several times before.'

'And—the accident—what happened?' Her inside shook as she waited for his reply.

He shrugged. 'We went to Kyoto together. Our firm has a textile side, as you may know, and we're interested in the silk industry there. Mariko's family lives in Kyoto and we all had a meal together. It was late when we came out of the restaurant and Steve was no doubt up on cloud nine. He stepped into the road and—well—the traffic in Japan is somewhat horrendous, as you may have noticed. He very nearly went under a bus before he could take avoiding action.'

'Oh!' Sue's inside turned over sickeningly. For a moment she could say nothing, then she leaned forward across the table. 'He *is* all right, isn't he? You'd tell me if there was anything really bad?' Her voice shook.

'Of course I would.' He sounded a trifle impatient now. 'The hospital seems extremely efficient and he's getting the very best care available—the company arranges insurance for its staff, of course. The doctor I saw speaks no English and I'm not particularly fluent in Japanese but we managed to communicate. They want to do some tests, to be on the safe side, but I gathered that apart from the arm fracture they don't suspect anything that will keep Steve in hospital more than two or three days. He was worrying about the wedding, of course, but I should think he'll be OK for the end of the week, albeit with one arm in a sling. That's about all I can tell you.'

Sue nodded and sat back. 'Thank you,' she said, and after a little pause she added, 'And thank you again for—for meeting me and—and everything.'

'My pleasure,' he said drily. His eyes moved down to her mouth and she felt the heat rush into her cheeks. His eyes creased with amusement. 'I nearly muffed the meeting at the airport, didn't I? But I don't think I could possibly have recognised you from Steve's description. He told me to look out for a pale, skinny kid with a crop of yellow hair and a mouth that couldn't say boo to a goose.'

Sue grinned. That sounded like Steve's brotherly description. 'I've changed a bit since he last saw me, four years ago.'

His eyes rested momentarily upon the soft swell of her breasts under her blouse. Then he said with a touch of irony, 'You're quite a grown-up young lady, aren't you? Nicely-endowed, too.'

Sue felt a warm disturbance inside her and she lowered her eyes.

Luke said in an off-hand way, 'I'm sorry if I was—less than courteous at the airport. In places like that you need to be on your guard.'

She laughed confusedly. 'Do I really look that kind of woman?'

His mouth was suddenly grim again. 'I very much doubt if there is "that kind of woman" these days. You can't tell by appearances.' Then he smiled, as if

he regretted his sudden change of tone. 'You're a very
pretty young lady, Sue, and I'm quite sure you can say
boo to any number of geese.'

'Oh, indeed I can, I've learned to say boo to several
hundred head of cattle and lots and lots of silly sheep
in the last four years. But don't let's talk about me, tell
me about plans, I can't wait to see Steve.' She met his
eyes doubtfully. 'Are you really going to take me to
Kyoto—wouldn't that be putting you to too much
trouble? If you see me on to the train I expect I could
find my way to the hospital on my own.'

His grey eyes were quizzical as he said, 'My word,
you're a very independent young woman. Is that how
they train you down under?'

'You're expected to pull your weight,' she said.

'And you always do what you're expected to do?'

'Sometimes,' Sue said shortly. She was merely
Steve's kid sister to this man, but she objected to
being patronised. 'And sometimes I don't. But you
haven't answered my question.'

His eyebrows lifted. 'So I haven't. The answer is
yes, I *am* going to take you to Kyoto. No, it wouldn't
be too much trouble as I have to go back there
anyway—and I hope that doesn't sound ungracious;
I'm sure your company will be delightful. I might add
that I very much doubt if you could find your way
around Kyoto alone.'

'Oh!' Sue's mouth drooped. 'Is it a very big place?
Not as big as Tokyo, surely?' She looked down
through the window, at the high concrete buildings
rising on every side, at the bewildering mass of traffic
and the crowds of hurrying figures.

He shrugged. 'Not quite, but I once spent half an
hour trying to cross the station in Kyoto. I know it a
bit better now but it's still a very big city.' He looked
keenly at her. 'You look disappointed—are you?'

Sue said rather awkwardly, 'Not really, it's just that—well, it isn't like I expected. I thought it would be somehow more—more Japanese.'

'All temples and rice fields and little wooden houses?' he mocked.

'Something like that,' Sue admitted. He had a knack of making her feel stupid.

'Oh, there are plenty of those too, once you get outside the cities. You'll see some of them while you're here.'

Sue's face clouded. 'Steve promised to take me on some sightseeing trips if there was time before the wedding. But of course he won't be able to now. He'll have to take it easy when he comes out of hospital.'

'Poor little Sue!' he said drily. 'We'll have to see what can be arranged. Meanwhile you can have your first taste of real Japanese scenery. On the *shinkansen*.'

Her eyebrows went up. 'The *what*?'

'*Shinkansen*—the unique Japanese super-train. The "bullet train", it's called because it shoots along at going on for two hundred miles an hour. I took the precaution of booking our seats when I arrived here yesterday, so we'd better be moving. Can you be ready in ten minutes?'

An hour and a half had passed. The 'bullet train' had rushed through the endless Tokyo suburbs, past the little houses all squashed together; past the factories and the hoardings and the maze of streets. Now it was out into the countryside, hurtling along at a tremendous speed.

Sue's eyes were fixed on the scene outside the carriage window. The long ruler-straight rows of rice plants, divided by glittering canals, were blurred in the foreground by the speed of the train. Women in blue trousers with white handkerchiefs round their hair, worked in groups. Here and there farm houses and wooden buildings, further from the railway line, passed out of view more slowly. And behind it all a line of mountains hazy in the mist, seemed not to move at all.

'Oh look,' she gasped. 'Isn't that Mount Fuji?' For a moment the unmistakable cone shape of the famous mountain seemed to hover, wraithlike, snowcapped, infinitely beautiful against the pale blue sky, before it disappeared again into the mist. 'Oh, it's gone,' she said in disappointment.

As soon as they had left Tokyo, Luke had opened his brief-case and taken out a wad of papers. Now he glanced briefly out of the window, eyebrows raised.

'I haven't been in a train since I left England,' Sue explained, 'and this is much more super than the trains I remember.' Her eyes were shining. 'It's all so fascinating.'

'The scenery comes up to your expectations, then?' he said absently, his attention returning to his papers.

'Oh, *yes*,' Sue breathed. 'It's exactly like the pictures in a book I've got. It's all so—so delicate and beautiful. So absolutely different from Australia.' She sighed with pleasure.

'Good,' he said. 'Well, you enjoy yourself while I get on with some work, OK?' He tapped the pile of papers.

Sue nodded and turned back to the window, and it seemed somehow appropriate that at that moment the train rushed into one of the long tunnels that it was to encounter on its route to Kyoto. Somehow the journey seemed to have lost a little of its first enchantment. Of course Luke must have seen it all before—many times perhaps—but it would have been nice if he had wanted to talk, perhaps to tell her something about Japan, which country he seemed to know quite well. It would have been better—so much better—if Steve had been here with her instead of this indifferent stranger.

Kyoto station was just as bewildering as the airport in Tokyo had been. 'You were quite right,' Sue panted, almost running to keep up with Luke's long strides as he led the way along passages and gangways and up steep steps, carrying her heavy bag with ease. 'I could never have tackled this on my own.'

Luke glanced down at her as a crowd of tourists jostled and pushed. 'Keep close to me,' he instructed tersely. 'I want to hand you over to Steve in one piece.' She could almost hear him thinking. 'And what a relief *that* will be,' and foolishly she let the thought hurt. What did she expect, for goodness' sake? That a man like Luke Masters would want to prolong his relationship with the ingenuous kid sister of a colleague, to whom he considered he owed a duty? The very idea was ludicrous.

When they finally emerged from the station Kyoto looked very much the same as Tokyo had done—a huge, busy city, teeming with people and traffic.

'We'll park your baggage at the hotel,' Luke said. 'You can have Steve's room at the New Miyako— that's where Steve and I are staying. It's very handy for the station; we can walk there.'

Sue had given up trying to take in her whereabouts, she simply followed where Luke led and eventually she found herself in another bewilderingly huge hotel, in another bedroom, almost identical to the one in Tokyo. She didn't even bother to look around. 'Can we go straight to the hospital now, please?' she asked Luke, twisting her fingers together nervously.

He put a hand on her shoulder as if to steady her. 'Don't panic,' he said. 'Nothing to be gained by getting in a flap.'

'I'm not getting in a flap,' she said with a sudden spurt of spirit. 'I just want to get to Steve.'

'OK,' he said shortly. 'I'll get you there.'

She looked up at his face, detached, unsmiling. He was quite obviously bored with her, but she had to rely on him to get her to Steve. And she *was* grateful, because he didn't have to help her. She was sorry she had spoken sharply. 'I know you will,' she said. 'I don't know what I should have done without you.' She grinned apologetically.

He looked down into her small face with its huge misty blue eyes, and suddenly his features relaxed and he almost smiled. 'That's what a man likes to hear. You can tell me more on the way to the hospital.'

His hand slipped from her shoulder to her elbow as they went out to the lift and she had an urgent desire to move nearer to him, to press her cheek against his shoulder, to feel his arm go round her. The touch of his hand was doing strange things to her composure; she didn't recognise herself as the self-possessed young woman who had said goodbye to Ross at Sydney Airport less than twenty-four hours ago. She really must try to get a grip on herself. Perhaps it was just the result of her nervous anxiety about Steve. Perhaps when she had seen him and reassured herself this weakness would pass. It would have to. In the lift she stood as far from Luke as she could.

Luke seemed to know his way about the hospital when they got there. Up stairs and along passages he strode with the confident step of a man who knows where he is going, and Sue, who by this time was feeling rather like a jelly that hasn't set properly, hurried along beside him. Finally he stopped outside a door with Japanese characters on it, tapped, and opened the door.

Inside, a nurse was sitting behind a desk; it was all

very neat and official-looking. She smiled as she saw
Luke and Sue wondered if that was a good sign, but
she was beginning to realise that in this country
everyone smiled most of the time, so she waited, her
heart beating very fast. Luke drew her forward and
said a few words in a strange, guttural, lilting language
that must be Japanese and the nurse smiled even more
widely and nodded her head towards Sue, who smiled
and nodded back helplessly. This was all a little
nightmarish, like being put on to a stage in a play
when you didn't know a word of your part.

Luke said, 'She says Steve is improving and we may
see him now for a short time. Come along, and don't
forget to bow your thanks to the sister. She'll approve
of that.'

Sue did as she was told and he also bowed and then
they were out in the corridor again. 'This is it, I
think,' he said. 'Steve's in a private room, the next one
along, the sister said. At least I think that's what she
said. I have to guess a good deal—the language isn't
easy.'

He opened a door a crack and peered round and
then he opened it wider and went inside. 'Hullo again,
Steve, how are you feeling today? You're looking
great. See who I've brought with me.'

Sue felt her limbs go weak. This was the moment
she had waited for for years and there was a great
lump in her throat and she couldn't put one foot in
front of the other. She felt Luke's hand on her arm
and then he was leading her towards the high bed and
there was Steve, his left arm hitched up in a strange
contraption, looking thinner and very pale but still
undoubtedly her own dear Steve.

Luke pulled up a chair for her. 'I'll wait outside for
you,' he said. Sue didn't notice his going out of the
room.

She sank into the chair. 'Steve,' she whispered, 'it's really you isn't it?'

They stared at each other in silence. It was totally unexpected and quite ridiculous to feel awkward with one's own brother. 'Steve . . .' she began, at the same moment that he said, 'Sue . . .'

They burst out laughing together and all the strangeness had suddenly gone and it was like slipping back into the old happy life. Her eyes passed eagerly over his face; he looked older and more serious than she remembered but there were still the laughter crinkles beside his blue eyes and his light brown hair was as unruly as ever.

'It's me all right, Sis.'

He grinned his lopsided grin and Sue said, 'I think I'm going to cry.' She groped in her pocket for a hanky and blew her nose hard. 'That's better. How are you, Steve? How do you feel, really and truly?'

'Not too bad,' he said. 'Not too bad, considering. They don't tell you much—and if they did I wouldn't understand what they were saying, I don't suppose. I can get by in the language usually, but I haven't yet learned all the medical terms.' He grinned and changed the subject.

'I can't believe you're really here, Sis.' Steve took her hand with his right hand and hung on to it. 'It's the funniest feeling, having a grown-up sister, and not at all bad-looking at that.' He pretended to examine her, head on one side. 'I don't think I'd have known you at first. Did Luke find you OK? It was really great of him to offer to meet you.'

Sue thought she heard a note of—what was it—admiration? deference? 'Yes, we found each other finally,' she said. 'He's been very—er—kind. He says he works with you.'

Steve pulled a face. 'Nice of him to put it like that. Actually he's the Big Boss, Sue. The one who holds my future in his hands. And last night he held my life in his hands.' He met her eyes soberly. 'That bloke saved me, Sue. He rushed into the road and pulled me back—if it hadn't been for him I'd have gone under that bus. He risked going under with me.'

She stared at him, wide-eyed. 'He didn't tell me.'

Steve said, 'Well, he wouldn't, would he? He's not that kind of chap. I only met him a couple of days ago myself, of course, but I've heard of him on the company grapevine. He's quite a fellow.' A touch of hero-worship now.

'Oh yes, quite,' Sue said in an offhand way.

She had never been able to hide her feelings from Steve, and now he gave her an old-fashioned look. 'Fancy him, do you, little sister? Don't get too carried away, I doubt if he's in the market again so soon—not with a six-month-old divorce behind him.'

'Ah!' breathed Sue, almost shocked by the sudden jubilation that ran through her body like wine. And that explained a lot of things too—his sudden moodiness, the cynical view of women that he didn't even try to hide. But she smiled at Steve. 'Don't worry, I'm not in his league—I'm just the kid sister. But now, tell me about everything. What about the wedding—will you be OK to walk down the aisle, or whatever they do in Japan?'

Steve's brow wrinkled for a moment, then cleared. 'I've damn well got to be. It would be a terrible blow for Mariko's family if it had to be put off. They've been up to their eyes in preparations for weeks. They take weddings very, very seriously out here. None of your slipping away to a register office. It's going to be a traditional ceremony, held at a Shinto shrine, here in Kyoto, and all Mariko's family will be there in force, down to the matriarch of the family, the great-grandmother, I understand.'

'And when do I meet Mariko?'

'Any moment now, she said she would look in this morning.' His voice softened, his eyes, as blue as her own, were bright. 'You'll like her, Sue, she's a wonderful girl is Mariko.'

Sue was watching her brother's face and what she saw there reassured her completely that he knew what he was doing in marrying a girl from a different race and culture. Steve was intelligent and adaptable and he was in love. The way he spoke Mariko's name told her that.

She pressed his hand warmly. 'I'm so glad for you, Steve. It's all splendid.'

He nodded. 'I think so. I'm glad you're happy about it. But I'm sorry I shan't be able to look after you and give you a good time, and there's so much for us to talk about after all these years, but I suppose it's no good trying to catch up now. We'll just have to wait and hope we get an opportunity later on.' He frowned worriedly. 'Meanwhile, Luke says he's booked you in at our hotel, so you should be comfortable there, and I'm sure he'll be somewhere around if you get bothered about anything.'

Right on cue, it seemed, Luke put his head round the door. 'The nurse says time's up.'

Sue got to her feet. 'See you soon then.' She kissed Steve. 'Will you be coming back to the hotel when they let you out?' She managed to keep her voice cheerful but it was an effort. Now that she had to leave Steve she began to feel rather depressed.

Steve pulled a rueful face. 'It's all a bit vague at the moment.' His face clouded. 'Oh Lord, this is so rotten for you, Sis, not at all how I planned it.'

Luke came up behind her. 'Don't worry, Steve, I'll

stand in for you. Not a very good substitute but perhaps Sue won't mind too much. I've arranged to visit Sakayo-ku this afternoon, to see Mr Yamaga about those silks. Sue can tag along if she likes.'

Steve looked relieved. 'That would be a splendid plan.' He smiled at both of them. 'You'll love the silks, Sue, they're really beautiful, right up your street.' He didn't seem to notice the patronising way that Luke had spoken. *Tag along*—that put her firmly back in the schoolroom.

Luke gripped Sue's arm and shepherded her to the door. 'That's fixed then, we'll be off.' He raised a hand in salute. 'Keep smiling, old boy. I'll bring Sue in to see you again very soon.'

'There,' he said when they were outside the room. 'Satisfied that Steve's not at death's door?'

'Yes, thank you.' She would *not* rise to his sarcasm.

But he wasn't listening and she saw that he had recognised a girl in a yellow dress who was tripping along the corridor towards them. She stopped when she saw Luke and then Sue found herself being introduced to Mariko.

'You are Steve's sister?' Mariko spaced her words carefully. 'How do you do?' She held out a cool little hand, Western-fashion.

Mariko was so pretty and dainty; her dark hair, parted in the middle, hung smoothly to her shoulders. Her ivory complexion was quite perfect; it really did look like a magnolia flower. Sue's first impulse was to give her new sister-in-law-to-be a hug and a kiss, but she wasn't sure if that was correct in this country where everything seemed so formal, so she took Mariko's hand, saying warmly, 'I'm so glad to meet you, Mariko. I'm sure we shall be great friends.'

Mariko bowed her head quietly. 'I hope you enjoy visit,' she said carefully. 'You have good journey?'

'Very good, thank you.' Sue eyed the Japanese girl doubtfully. It was a stiff little exchange between two people who would soon be part of the same family, and she felt a little chilled.

Mariko turned to Luke. 'I go to see Steve,' she said firmly.

'Of course.' Luke turned back along the corridor. 'You'll find him looking much better today.'

They accompanied Mariko to the door of the room they had just left and parted with bows and polite smiles. Luke closed the door behind the Japanese girl and he and Sue started on their way out of the hospital once more.

'Oh dear.' Sue's small face was rueful. 'I don't think Mariko liked the look of me very much.'

'Rubbish.' Luke dismissed her doubts impatiently. 'You really mustn't be so touchy. Probably Mariko is thinking the very same thing about you at this moment. The Japanese have a certain restraint, you know. Coming from an extrovert country like Australia you'll find it strange at first. Anyway, we never know what people are thinking about us so it's a waste of time speculating. Now, for God's sake cheer up, girl, and let's go and find ourselves some lunch.'

Sue walked along in silence beside him. She would have liked to say something about his saving Steve—to thank him—but she couldn't think how to put it into words. So she just said apologetically, 'Yes, I am being rather wet, aren't I? I'm sorry.' She added a little shyly, 'I didn't realise—Steve told me that you're the Big Boss—that was how he put it—and in the circumstances you must be bored to tears with me. You've been very kind but now I really can't be a burden on you any longer. If you'll just put me into a taxi to go back to the hotel I can stay there quite happily until Steve contacts me. Some of the staff seem to speak English so I won't need to starve,' she added cheerfully. 'And I'm not really as helpless as I must have appeared to you up to now. I can usually look after myself quite well.'

She glanced up at him at the end of this speech and saw a quirk of amusement at the corners of his long mouth. 'Have you quite finished?' he said, 'because I know a good restaurant where we could eat. Come along and you shall be introduced to real Japanese food.' He took her arm in a firm grasp and bundled her into a passing taxi, which stopped as he hailed it.

Well, she'd said her say, she'd offered him a get-out, there wasn't any more she could do. Sue felt a little thrill of excitement at the thought of spending an afternoon with Luke, instead of sitting alone in her hotel.

They reached the restaurant after a short taxi-ride and Luke paused, looking in at the window. Sue said doubtfully, 'Oh, how odd to put the actual cooked food in the window. It doesn't seem very hygienic.'

Luke grinned. 'Look a bit closer. You're not expected to eat that—it's a wax model—quite a work of art, don't you agree?'

'I don't believe it.' Sue peered into the window, where a handleless pan contained a marvellous selection of vegetables—leeks, onions, mushrooms, with thin slices of meat and transparent noodles. They were so tempting and crisp-looking that it was almost impossible to believe that they were just models. 'All right, I'll take your word for it, but I still feel tempted to take a bite out of one of those mushrooms.'

'Don't you dare,' he said. 'Behave yourself, young woman, and don't disgrace me.'

He was fooling of course, but at the same time he was putting her down, reminding her of their difference in age and status. But Sue was feeling more

like herself now that she was reassured about Steve.
More like the Sue who had held her own for four
years among the workers on a large cattle station.
She certainly wasn't going to let herself be crushed
by any Luke Masters, important though he might
consider himself. Everything in Japan was new and
fascinating' she wasn't going to pretend to be blasé
about it.

They entered the restaurant. '*Tatami* mats on the
floor.' Luke pointed out the spotless pale-green
matting. 'That means shoes off.'

They left their shoes side by side and put on the
sandals that were provided. Sue tried to imagine
Auntie Meg persuading the cattle-workers to take off
their boots when they came into the house for a
meal—and failed. 'What a good idea,' she said. 'And
what a lot of work it must save.'

The room was large and cool, the low tables widely
spaced. Sue watched as Luke ordered their meal by
the simple means of pointing to the wax models of
food in the window. '*Sukiyaki,*' he told Sue. 'It's one
of the great dishes of Japan, and I should guess that
they probably don't serve anything else here.'

They sank down on to cushions beside a table about
the height of a coffee table. Luke, who was obviously
quite accustomed to all this, sat cross-legged and Sue
sat back on her heels as she had seen Japanese women
do in pictures in her books. It wasn't very comfortable
but she told herself she must get used to it.
Immediately a waitress in a pretty flowered kimono
placed a small tray before each of them, bowing low as
she did so. On the tray she put a bowl of green tea and
a steaming hot towel rolled up in a little basket.
Another waitress brought a neat little gas cooker and
placed it on the table. Then, kneeling before them, her
kimono draped around her, she proceeded to cook

small pieces of food, serving each piece to them as it was ready.

Sue watched all this, absorbed, her lips apart, her eyes shining. But when she glanced at Luke she saw that he was watching her with an ironic smile hovering about his mouth. Patronising brute, she thought, and she said calmly, 'This is wonderful. I really feel I'm in Japan now. I expect you're quite *au fait* with it all so you must please guide me about the right thing to do.'

'A pleasure,' he said, and his eyes were faintly mocking. She knew he was seeing through her assumed meekness. 'Have you used chopsticks before? No? Well, this is the drill.' He tore the paper cover from a pair of chopsticks and placed them between her fingers. 'No, not like that—this way.'

It was quite ridiculous—just the touch of his hand on hers made her fingers feel like thumbs and her heartbeat quicken. She pulled away. 'OK, I get the idea,' she muttered, glancing round at occupants of the other tables—mostly Japanese men in dark suits who were handling their chopsticks with ease, picking up each morsel of food as it was delivered to them by the cook, dipping it into the little bowls on their trays and transferring it to their mouths with the economy of effort born of a lifetime's experience.

She pushed his hand away. 'I can manage,' she said, trying desperately to grab a piece of mushroom with the business ends of the chopsticks. But each time she grabbed, the wretched things slipped and twisted and the ends crossed over each other and the mushroom slithered down into her bowl. She tried again and again with no better result, only too aware of Luke's cool look of amusement.

Finally she was defeated. 'You can't even spear the bits with this blunt instrument,' she wailed, her cheeks pink with effort and annoyance. 'Can't you ask them for a fork or something?'

He was laughing aloud at her now. 'Poor little Sue. It was you who wanted to sample the real Japanese way of life, remember? Don't be such an independent little cuss. Let me show you.'

Again his hand closed round hers and again his touch set off firecrackers exploding inside her. 'Now look.' He demonstrated with exaggerated patience. 'Hold one stick anchored with *this* finger and work the other one—*so*, making them into a pair of pincers. Bravo, you've done it.'

As she nibbled the morsel of mushroom she had managed to convey to her mouth Sue felt as weak as if she had been fighting a battle—and in a way she *had*. Against herself. She told herself that it was humiliating and absurd that she should allow Luke Masters to have this shattering effect on her. Body chemistry, they called it, and it could happen to anyone. She must just be careful to avoid any physical contact with him in the time they were together. Otherwise she would be in danger of making an utter fool of herself.

As the meal progressed Sue got more and more expert with the chopsticks and by the time it was almost over she was managing—rather clumsily, but still managing—to pick up thin slivers of newly cooked meat and dip them in the little bowl of beaten egg on her tray, so that they sizzled deliciously.

'This is super.' She lifted shining blue eyes to Luke's. 'Is all Japanese food as good as this?'

He looked into her eyes and it was a moment or two before he replied. Then he said rather quickly, 'Some is even better. Some, I'd guess, you won't like at all. My favourite is *tempura*—I have a weakness for the seafood bits, particularly the scampi. We'll go to a *tempura* restaurant next time we eat.'

Sue took a sip of the warm *sake*. It seemed strange to drink warm wine (though she wasn't very accustomed to drinking wine of any sort) but she found she was enjoying it more as the meal went on. 'Do the restaurants only serve one particular dish?'

'Most of them have their own specialities,' he told her, 'so if both parties share the same taste it makes for a peaceful evening out. Otherwise it's liable to turn into a Jack Spratt situation in reverse.'

'What's that?' Sue took another drink of *sake*, watching her companion's face with a fascination of which she was totally unaware.

'Don't you know the old nursery rhyme?' He quoted solemnly,

'Jack Spratt could eat no fat, his wife could eat no lean,
And so between the two, you see, they licked the platter clean.'

'How convenient for a married couple,' Sue laughed. 'It would save on the food bills.' She was beginning to feel a little lightheaded. Perhaps it was the *sake*, or maybe sitting here with Luke Masters beside her was having an intoxicating effect on her. 'Although the cat couldn't get much in the way of left-overs.'

Suddenly he wasn't smiling. In fact he didn't seem to have heard her little joke. 'Unfortunately married couples have more important things to disagree about than food. Many more,' he added bleakly.

Oh dear, everything seemed to lead back to the same place—his disgruntlement about marriage. She wondered what his wife had been like to leave him so embittered. Had she left him for another man? Or had she just found him impossible to live with? Perhaps they had disagreed and quarrelled about everything? She knew some couples who nagged at each other all the time. They sometimes seemed to get a kick out of it. But she wouldn't think Luke Masters would enjoy arguing—especially with a woman. He would expect to be the dominant partner.

She decided not to care if Luke was moody and touchy—that was his problem. And she decided, too, not to try to act the kind of girl that he would be accustomed to taking around with him—sophisticated, experienced. She was thrilled and excited to be seeing Japan—Steve's Japan—the Japan she had dreamed about ever since Steve came to live and work here, and she didn't care if she showed it. And if Luke Masters wanted to treat her like a small child being taken on an outing, what did that matter? Being in Japan, drinking in the atmosphere, was what mattered, and already, as they left the restaurant, she was beginning to get the feel of this fabulous oriental country—so utterly different from anything she'd known in her life up to now.

They got into a taxi again—taxis seemed to spring up everywhere among the busy traffic—and drove to Sakayo-ku. Sue kept on firing questions at Luke, which he answered with commendable patience, and he told her that *ku* meant 'district'. Here they visited a huge building, rather like a warehouse on several floors, all crammed with silks and kimonos and pottery and fancy goods: exquisite little purses, lacquered boxes, tea bowls and rice bowls, embroidered belts and tiny posies of flowers. Sue's eyes grew larger and more fascinated as they walked around.

On each floor there was a space where craftsmen were at work and Sue tugged at Luke's arm to stop him so that they could watch an artist painting a green bamboo branch on a sheet of wafer-thin paper, his brush moving with quick, sure strokes and the minimum of fuss. In another place there was a young man painting a landscape on a bowl, and in yet another two girls embroidering in glowing silks, their fingers moving so quickly and accurately that Sue stood watching with amazement. She could have stayed for ages, and it would be nice to buy some little present to take back to Auntie Meg, but Luke's hand was firmly on her arm now, urging her away.

'Sorry to spoil the fun but business calls,' he said. 'I have an appointment and it's considered very impolite to be late for an appointment in Japan. You'd better come along with me,' he added. 'I wouldn't want to lose you among the pretty-pretties.'

She felt like coming back at him with, 'You can claim me at the lost children department,' but then she remembered how much she owed this man. If it hadn't been for him Steve might have been . . . a cold shiver passed through her. The least you can do, Sue Larkin, she scolded herself, is not to make a nuisance of yourself. So she trailed along after him and sat and twiddled her thumbs while he interviewed a small Japanese man with slicked-back hair and thick glasses and the inevitable dark business suit, in a tiny box of an office on the top floor.

The interview went on and on. The elderly man seemed to speak a little halting English and Luke was doing his best with Japanese, but Sue could tell that there were serious difficulties in communication.

At last the enterview ended with much bowing and smiling and they were out in the street again. Luke was, Sue thought, more than a little put out about something.

'Wasn't it satisfactory?' she ventured.

'As far as it went,' he said. He stood still for a moment, frowning, obviously deep in thought. Picture of tycoon making decision, Sue thought with an inward giggle.

Then he said, 'I can't finalise anything by staying here. We'll have to go further afield. A trip into the Japanese countryside,' he added. 'That's what you wanted, wasn't it?' His dark eyebrows raised themselves ironically.

'But—but . . .' Sue faltered. 'You don't *have* to take me with you to . . . wherever you're going.'

He brought his attention back to her as they stood in the sunshine, with crowds of people jostling round them. His eyes were narrowed as he looked down at her with that now-familiar expression of amused tolerance.

'No, little girl, I don't have to,' he said smoothly. 'But I'm going to, all the same. I'm not leaving you on your own in Kyoto, so you'll have to come along with me. We'll get back in time to see Steve this evening if that's what you're worrying about. Come on, let's be on our way.' He hailed a passing taxi.

The taxi pulled up beside them and Sue moved forward. At the same moment the door shot open and rapped her smartly on the head. She reeled back and found herself in Luke's arms. 'Wh—what happened?' she croaked. He half lifted, half pushed her into the taxi and she collapsed back against the seat. 'Silly child, haven't you noticed that the drivers here open the doors by remote control?' he scolded. 'Are you hurt?'

She rubbed her head. 'No, of course not.' She tried to sound dignified but she was terribly conscious that his arm was still holding her.

He shouted something to the driver and the taxi

moved off, weaving through the maze of traffic. 'You're too impulsive, you want to watch what you're doing in a strange country.' Luke sounded like a stern schoolmaster. 'You might have been seriously hurt.'

'I'm sorry,' Sue said meekly. 'I seem to need a bodyguard.'

'You certainly do.' To her confusion his arm tightened round her and he added amusedly, 'And a very nice little body to guard, it is too.'

She looked up and his eyes were glinting with laughter in the dimness inside the taxi. Something leapt inside her and her mouth went dry and she couldn't think of a thing to say.

Oh, she thought dazedly, let him kiss me, please let him kiss me, and she waited, holding her breath. He had kissed her before—'to begin her education' he'd said—perhaps he would do it again. She didn't care if he was merely humouring her, laughing at her, she just ached to feel his mouth on hers again.

But he didn't kiss her. Instead he lowered his head and rested his cheek against her hair. The something that had leaped inside Sue settled down into a feeling of sensuous delight, as if she were floating on a warm sea, rising and dipping with the tide.

The taxi continued on its death-defying way through the maze of traffic, missing other vehicles, not to mention cyclists, by what seemed like a tenth of an inch. At any other time Sue would have been hanging on to the edge of her seat in fright. But now she noticed nothing. She was facing a sudden and heart-stopping question.

Was this new overpowering sensation that she felt inside herself really love, or was it just an overdue adolescent crush? Was she falling in love with Luke Masters? Or was she just bemused by Japan and the novelty and excitement of everything that was happening? And by the disturbing masculinity of the man himself?

She wished she knew the answer.

CHAPTER THREE

LUKE said, 'You won't want to sit through another endless meeting, listening to me struggling with my Japanese. Let's find somewhere pleasant under the trees where you can sit and wait for me. Then we'll work out where we can eat this evening.'

They had travelled in a bus to this spot outside Kyoto and it was lovely to be out in the country after the bustle of the town. They walked together along a rough road between fields of rice, tawny-yellow and looking ready for the harvest. Further on were plots of vegetables, cabbage and lettuce. Every square foot of land capable of producing food was used, Luke told her. 'Japan is very clever with her agriculture. When the rice is harvested they will grow crops of wheat and barley on the same fields.'

He seemed to know a great deal about the Japanese way of life. Sue listened as he talked on, but she hardly took in what he was saying about farming. She looked up at him, striding along beside her, his dark hair blowing back in the breeze, his bronzed skin pulled tightly over high cheekbones, his nose and mouth finely-chiselled in profile. He had a Red Indian look, she thought, proud, arrogant, sublimely sure of himself. She turned her head away quickly, because he was so sensational, and just looking at him turned her bones to water.

They reached the end of the rice-field and here Luke stopped. 'This must be the place,' he said. Before them was a shallow stream where great lengths of patterned silk lay spread out on the pebbles in the

water. Women were bending over it, turning it this
way and that and the water of the stream was streaked
with scarlet and green and yellow as the excess dye
was washed out of the silk. Men in happi coats were
tenderly lifting another length from the water and
arranging it along the bank of the stream to dry,
chattering to each other in their strange, rather
guttural language. They paused in their task as Luke
and Sue passed, sinking on their knees to bow nearly
to the ground. Luke bowed back. 'They guess I'm on
my way to see their boss. This is a great place for
boosting one's ego,' he grinned. 'I shall begin to feel
quite important soon.'

'Well, you *are* important, aren't you?' Sue smiled up
at him under long, silky lashes. 'The Big Boss, Steve
called you. The one who makes everyone else feel small.'

His eyes narrowed against the sun as he glanced
down at her. 'I don't make you feel small, surely, Sue?
Not a girl who's held her own in the tough Aussie
world?'

She laughed. 'You make me feel positively micro-
scopic.' She was fooling, but it was unfortunately true.
There weren't any men like Luke Masters in the
world where she had been living for the past four
years. Tough men—yes—attractive in a sturdy, rugged
way. Honest, straightforward. Men like Ross Stevens.
But Luke Masters was something quite different, and
none of those men had quickened her breathing and
turned her knees to jelly as he did.

He joined in her laughter and put an arm through
hers as they walked on along the rough, grassy track.
'I don't believe a word of it,' he said. 'Look—those are
mulberry trees, the silkworms feed on mulberry
leaves. You're right in the middle of one of the oldest
industries in the world now. Even the little silk-worms
are working away like mad.'

'And never seeing the beauty they are helping to make,' Sue sighed. 'It's worse than working on a production line. Oh look,' she stopped, drawing in her breath, 'there's a lake, how absolutely super. I haven't seen a lake for years.'

'You're partial to lakes?'

'I love them. How clever of you to find a lake for me.' She laughed up at him.

'We aim to please,' The hardness had gone from Luke's mouth as he looked down at the small, eager face, at the sparkle in the blue eyes, at the way Sue's lint-fair hair curved into her slender neck. 'You can sit and admire your lake while I go and argue with Mr Sato over there.' He pointed towards a group of wooden buildings nestling under a hill. 'OK?'

'OK.' Sue watched him stride away, a little smile on her lips. Before he reached the nearest of the wooden buildings he turned and waved and she waved back. Suddenly, for no particular reason, their relationship seemed to have changed. He no longer seemed like a busy executive, carrying out a boring social duty. They were friends, he had accepted her. She saw it in his expression, heard it in his voice.

Sue looked up at the washed blue sky, at the bank of pine trees beyond which the water of the lake glistened in the autumn sunshine. She spread out her arms and took a deep, deep breath of the clear country air. Then, with a little whoop of pleasure she galloped across the humpy grass towards the beckoning water that glistened in the sunshine.

She crossed a wooden bridge, where the stream ran into the lake, and found a place to sit, under a tree. From here she could see Luke when he emerged from his business meeting. It was very quiet and rather beautiful here. On the opposite side of the lake a bank of maple-trees were just beginning to turn

colour, flaming patches against the darker green of
the pines. In the far distance the mountains rose,
brooding over everything. There were very few
people around; several men were moving about at
the far end of the lake working some wooden
contraption in the water. Something to do with the
silk, she supposed. The chuckle of the stream,
running fast over its pebbles, the occasional chirp of
an unseen bird, the smell of the pines. It was all so
peaceful . . . so *familiar*.

Sue closed her eyes, leaning back against the rough
bark of a tree trunk and suddenly memory touched
her, vague at first then piercing clear until this place in
rural Japan disappeared and she was back at home in
England's Lake District, running across the grass
towards the place where her father had set up his
easel.

'Hi there, I've brought us a picnic. Can you bear to
stop working?' Her arm was flung round him, her
cheek rubbing against his shoulder, affectionate as a
puppy. She could feel again the rough texture of the
brown tweed jacket that he wouldn't be parted from,
the straying lock of soft fair hair that tickled her
forehead.

'Oh, I *like* that.' She stood back and examined the
picture that he was painting. Daddy called these
pictures his pot-boilers—small views of local scenery
that sold readily to summer visitors and helped to pay
the bills when the income from his part-time lecturing
dried up in the long summer vacation.

But Sue loved them. And now, sitting here in Japan,
she was back again in her childhood. She saw quite
clearly again the picture on the easel. A water-colour,
three-quarters finished. A corner of the lake, a water
bird skimming the surface, the pine trees, the hills.
She was living it again—that last summer before her

life crashed into fragments. Never once, in Australia, had she allowed herself to brood on the past for long. Daddy wouldn't have wanted her to, he would have told her always to stack away the pictures that are finished with their faces to the wall, and start on a new one with hope and confidence. That had been his way of putting it, his philosophy of life, right up to the time he'd gone out that freezing winter night with the mountain rescue team.

For four years she had lived that philosophy as best she could, but now the past came pouring back into her memory, not to be resisted. The low, white cottage in the glen; the swing in the garden; the wooden steps that Daddy had built into the apple tree so that she could climb up and dream among the branches; the sturdy little car that deposited her at school each day and picked her up each afternoon. She could hear the chattering as the children all came tumbling out, pushing and giggling, waving and running as they spotted their parents' cars. She could see Daddy in his old, beloved tweed jacket sitting behind the wheel of the little black car, a pipe jutting out of his mouth, so dear, so understanding. The evenings in the little living room, poring over homework, books spread out on the round table with its tasselled chenille cloth, while Daddy sat reading by the fire, Bob, the elderly sheepdog, snoring gently at his feet. Friends to tea, birthday parties, the joy of Steve coming home from university, the long treks across the fells— It was all there again as vivid as if it had never ended and she knew now with certainty that she had put down no new roots in Australia.

'Hullo, Sue. Have I been too long?'

Sue opened her eyes, blinking stupidly as Luke appeared, towering above her.

'Been asleep?'

'No, I—I was . . .' It had been so real and now it had gone. She bit her lip as tears flooded into her eyes. She jerked her head away. 'I'm sorry, I . . .' She groped for a handkerchief and blew her nose hard. 'Is it time to go?' She started to struggle to her feet but he pushed her back, sinking down on to the grass beside her.

'What's the matter, little Sue? Is it Steve? He's going to be OK, I promise you.'

She shook her head. 'No, it's not Steve. It was just this place—it reminded me . . .' She grinned faintly. 'I guess I just got homesick.'

'Homesick? Here?' Luke looked baffled as his glance took in the lake, the trees, the hills. 'I can't imagine anything less like what I've seen of North Queensland, but of course . . .'

She shook her head. 'No—not Australia. I don't really think of Australia as home. I doubt if I ever will.'

'I was under the impression that you and Steve both came from Australia. Where is home then?'

'England,' she said rather shortly. 'The Lake District.' She didn't want to talk about it, to spoil the dream. But the dream was already fading and she was suddenly overcome with a most potent sadness. She bit her lip hard, her head turned away from him.

Luke said gently, 'Tell me about it,' but she shook her head mutely.

After a moment, he put a finger under her chin and turned her head towards him. 'Go on,' he said. 'Tell me.'

She stared up into his strong face, her eyes glazed with tears, and suddenly it all came pouring out—the heartache that had been dammed up inside her for four years, never really acknowledged, the longing for the home she never expected to see again. The words tumbled over each other and once begun she could hardly stop for breath. She told him about her father and what he had meant to her, about the mother she could only remember dimly, about the white cottage in the glen, about her own wish to be an artist like her father, about Steve's success at university and his ambitions. 'He had worked so hard and he had just been offered this job here in Japan. He was so thrilled and—and we were all so—so happy.' Her voice choked, failed.

'And then your father died?' he prompted quietly. 'Steve told me you had lost your father four years ago. That's about all I know of your family.'

'Yes.' Sue looked down at her hands, the fingers lacing in and out. 'We had to decide what to do. Steve couldn't take me to Japan with him and we had no relatives in England and he wouldn't hear of me staying alone. Then my aunt and uncle offered me a home in Australia.'

'You were——?'

'I was sixteen, nearly seventeen. I'd just started at art school in Lancaster.'

Luke nodded. 'Quite a problem you must have had, both of you.'

Sue said, 'It wasn't really. At first Steve said he'd turn down the job and we'd stay on together but of course I couldn't let him do that. So I accepted their offer.'

'Very self-sacrificing of you!'

The irony in his voice jerked Sue back to reality. She had thought he was listening with understanding and all the time he must have been bored by her emotional outpourings. 'There's no need to be sarcastic,' she flared, angry and hurt.

'Oh dear, I'm sorry, Sue. I'm afraid I have a bad habit of cynicism. I put it on like protective clothing. But I should have known better than to use it on you. Forgive me?' He unlaced her fingers and took both hands in his. 'Please go on. You went to Australia?'

She looked doubtfully at him, wanting to believe him, the now-familiar churning inside starting up at his touch. After a moment she nodded. 'Yes, I went to Australia, where I've been for the last four years. End of story.'

'Not quite the end,' Luke said. 'You're still longing to go back to your roots.'

She nodded. 'Oh yes, I am,' she said fervently. 'But I feel bad about it. It seems so ungrateful when my aunt and uncle have been so good to me—given me a home—made me part of their family. And I love them very much.'

Luke looked out over the smooth water of the lake to the fringe of pine trees and the hills beyond. 'Yes, I can see what you mean about this place. Some peoples' roots are very strong and yours are the kind that don't transplant satisfactorily, that's what it is.'

Sue sighed. 'I suppose you're right.'

'You've never thought of going back, now that you're grown up? How old are you, Sue?'

'Twenty,' she said. 'Nearly twenty-one. No, I've never even considered it. How could I go back? I've no relatives in England. I haven't any money of my own, not even enough for the fare. And I'd have nowhere to go even if I could get there.' She grinned faintly. 'I'm afraid I'm not the enterprising sort of modern girl who hitchhikes round the world.'

He looked down at her tear-washed blue eyes, her vulnerable mouth. 'Poor little Sue,' he said softly.

She didn't want his pity. She went on more firmly, 'And I certainly couldn't walk out on my aunt and uncle just like that. Or on . . .' She stopped.

'Or on—who else?' There was a mile in his voice. 'Who is he?

'You're quite a thought-reader, aren't you?' Sue said crossly. 'OK, you may as well know it all. His name's Ross and he's the head stockman at the station where my uncle is book-keeper. Ross is coming up to forty; his wife died a few years ago, and . . .'

'And he thinks he might like a new young wife? You?'

She looked helplessly at him but her anger was forgotten now as she saw the way his mouth twitched, saw the laughter lines beside his eyes. She hadn't thought he had a sense of humour but now she was changing her mind.

'Who's telling this story?' A dimple showed in her cheek. 'Well, my aunt and uncle think it would be a good match for me.'

'But you don't?' he said quickly.

'Of course I do. It would be a splendid match. I'd have my own house—enough money—and I know that Ross is fond of me. And I—I like him very much. He's a nice man.'

Luke gave her a sideways look. 'H'm, it doesn't sound like a recipe for a wildly exciting marriage,' he drawled.

That was exactly what had been troubling Sue for weeks past so her voice was edged defensively as she came back with, 'Excitement isn't everything in marriage.'

A change seemed to come over Luke. He stood up and pulled her to her feet. 'You're so right,' he said in a flat weary voice. 'Come along, we must get going or we'll miss our train and then we'll be too late to visit Steve. I expect you'd like to look in at the hospital again this evening?'

★ ★ ★

They found Steve lying back in bed looking rather tired. 'They won't tell me when I can leave,' he grumbled. 'Mariko's been here trying to get it out of them but all they say is—in effect—wait and see. I've got to have time to get myself organised before the wedding. I haven't even ordered my suit yet,' he added glumly.

'Take it easy, son,' Luke soothed. 'I'll get you to the church—correction, shrine—on time. That's what a best man is for. You may not call it a "best man" in Japan but the idea's the same, I bet.'

Steve grinned at him and relaxed a little. 'OK, I'll rely on you.' He looked at Sue, sitting beside the bed and then back to Luke, standing at the foot of it. 'It seems the Larkin family is very much in your debt at present, Luke. First you pull me out from under a bus, then you take my little sister under your wing.' He pulled a wry face. 'How do we get around to making it up to you?'

Luke laughed easily. 'We'll think of some way. The firm will devise some really tricky jobs for you when you're back in circulation. Meanwhile, things are going pretty well. I've managed to get Mr Sato to give us first choice of his new patterns—and they're excellent. Just what we need. Tomorrow I'm off to Osaka to try and clinch the deal with Kimura and after that my business trip's all sewn up.' He glanced at Sue doubtfully. 'I don't know if you'd enjoy Osaka particularly. It's very much an industrial jungle.'

Sue was just about to assure him as coolly as she could that of course he needn't consider taking her along with him when Steve cut in with, 'No problem—Sue is invited to spend tomorrow at Mariko's home. Her mother is very anxious to meet Sue. You'd like that, would you, Sis?'

'Oh yes, I'd *love* to get to know Mariko and her

family,' Sue enthused. 'How kind of them to invite me.' Not for the world would she let Luke guess that the prospect of a whole day spent without seeing him stretched ahead like an empty eternity.

'That's settled then,' Luke said in a satisfied kind of voice. He must be glad to be rid of the responsibility of having her trailing round after him, of listening to her moans about living in Australia. Oh, why had she gone on and on about it? Sue thought miserably. He must have been bored with her stupid emotional outpourings. She hardly listened as Steve and Luke went on to talk business about Luke's trip to Osaka. She was almost beginning to wish she hadn't come to Japan after all; she was just a spare part and a nuisance to everyone.

In which uncharacteristically negative frame of mind Sue returned to the hotel with Luke. It made it even worse that Luke seemed more than usually pleased with life. 'Where would you like to eat this evening?' he enquired as they went up in the lift. 'In the restaurant here or shall we go out and find a convivial spot?'

They reached the door of Sue's room. 'Would you mind very much if I didn't join you?' she said rather formally. Of course, he wouldn't mind, he'd probably heave a long sigh of relief. 'I've got rather a headache and I'd really rather have a tray of something in my room and a very early night.'

'Oh dear, you're not really ailing, are you?' He sounded quite concerned. Of course, he wouldn't want to be saddled with her if she were going to be ill, that would be the bitter end.

She managed to produce a smile. 'No, really. I'm just rather tired. I'll be fine after a night's sleep.'

He followed her into her room. 'Poor little Sue—all this trekking around has been too much for you. I'll ask them to bring you up some supper, and you just take it easy. I'll be leaving early tomorrow morning so I won't disturb you. Mariko will pick you up here about eleven—that's what Steve arranged. Don't forget to take along some little gifts for the family—the Japanese are great on giving and receiving presents as you'll find out. You can get what you need in the hotel shopping arcade.'

Sue had sunk into a chair and he stood looking down at her, frowning. 'You'll be OK?'

'Of course,' she said rather stiffly. 'I wish you wouldn't feel so—so responsible for me.'

He was silent for a few moments, then he put a hand on her shoulder. 'It's rather odd,' he said amusedly, 'but I find I rather enjoy looking after you, Sue.'

She raised wide blue eyes to his and felt suddenly confused. 'In other words I'm pretty dim,' she said. 'I must be a real boost to your ego.'

He smiled. 'You're very sweet,' he said. 'Good night, little girl.' He bent down and dropped a kiss on her soft hair. 'Sleep well.'

'I will,' Sue said brightly, but as she watched him close the door she wondered if you could settle down to sleep when you had a small fire kindling inside you.

A small fire that threatened to turn into a blaze at any moment.

Some time around two o'clock in the morning, after tossing and turning for hours, the practical commonsense that Sue had somehow been absorbing in Australia surfaced. It was ridiculous, she scolded herself, to lie awake dreaming romantic dreams of the first sophisticated, worldly man she had ever met. She was simply going to spoil what should be a marvellous holiday—and could be still, in spite of poor Steve's accident. She would enjoy her day with Mariko tomorrow and not spend a single second yearning after Luke and wishing she was with him. Having arrived at that sensible conclusion, she got up and swilled her face and brushed her hair and, feeling better, went back to bed and fell asleep.

She spent the earlier part of next morning in the hotel shopping arcade. Most of the goods on display— fashionable Western-style clothes, jewellery, cameras and radios, as well as the fabulous Japanese kimonos, were very beautiful and wildly expensive and after doing some mental arithmetic, Sue reckoned she could easily spend all the supply of yen she had brought with her on a couple of small presents.

But Luke (Luke again, bother the man!) had said it was the 'done thing' to take presents to Mariko's family, and Luke seemed to know about Japanese customs. And eventually she had found a stall that specialised in small gifts. Mercifully the sales girl understood English and Sue emerged with a carrier full of little boxes, all exquisitely wrapped in pretty coloured paper and tied with fluffy bows. Sweets, dried seaweed, chopstick-rests shaped like fans, tiny wooden dolls for Mariko's two younger sisters, a little picture book for her brother. Pleased with her purchases, she found her way to the hotel foyer and sat down to wait for Mariko.

It was close on twelve o'clock when Mariko arrived and Sue had been sitting waiting in the hotel foyer, her eyes on the entrance, for what seemed like hours, working hard at not thinking about Luke and wondering what he was doing in Osaka and if he had given her a thought since last night.

She got up and went quickly towards the Japanese girl. Mariko was looking prettier than ever today, her

ivory cheeks had a faint pink flush that owed nothing
to make-up and her long, dark eyes were luminous.
She was wearing jeans and a casual scarlet sweater and
Sue wondered if she herself looked too dressed-up in
her blue suit and frilly white blouse, but she had little
else to choose from. Auntie Meg had bought her
clothes for the trip from a mail-order catalogue. The
blue suit and a couple of blouses, a warm jumper, and
a padded jacket, 'in case it turns cold', and a celery-
green jersey dress, the shade of green that comple-
mented her ash-blonde hair, to wear at the wedding,
'that'll be useful later on, when you go out'.

When you go out with Ross, she had meant. To the
small town, twenty miles away, to a cinema or a dance.
Ross had been inviting her out much more often
lately. Sue sighed now as she walked across the foyer
to greet Mariko. She didn't want to remember Ross
while she was here in Japan. Some time when she got
back she would have to make up her mind, but not
now.

Mariko was breathing quickly. 'So sorry—I am
late—I have been with Steve. He talk about coming
from hospital tomorrow. He is very excited and I stay
to talk with him. Are you angry because you have to
wait?'

Sue laughed. 'Of course I'm not angry, and it's
wonderful news about Steve. Hullo, Mariko, it's
lovely to see you.' Forgetting all about formalities she
leaned forward and kissed the other girl on the cheek.
For a moment Mariko looked startled then she gave
Sue a wide shy smile. 'You like to see shops, yes? We
go to my house afterwards.'

'That would be lovely,' Sue said.

'But first we eat,' Mariko said. 'Best to go early.'

Sue saw what she meant when they got to a snack-
bar in the shopping part of the town. This was very

different from the elegant Japanese restaurant where she had lunched with Luke—hot and crowded and people queuing up for seats. The two girls sat on high stools at the counter and munched hamburgers and drank coffee.

'I come here because it near my shop,' Mariko explained. 'I work in big store. I leave last week because of wedding.' She flushed prettily.

'You won't go on working after you're married?' Sue enquired and Mariko nodded her head, which, after a moment's confusion, Sue realised meant No and not Yes. 'Steve not wish it. I look after apartment in Tokyo and cook and wash and buy food. I am housewife,' she ended. 'In Japan wife do what husband say.' She smiled and her perfect teeth were like peeled almonds. 'If we live in UK will be different. I am more . . .' she groped for a word '. . . more *me*,' she ended triumphantly.

Sue laughed. 'Perhaps you're right,' she said. Although she couldn't quite see the gentle Mariko as an ardent feminist. But of course she hadn't met any ardent feminists, except in books. The Womens' Movement hadn't reached Langeroo. 'Tell me about how you met Steve,' she said impulsively. 'We're almost sisters and there is so much I don't know.'

Mariko's sloe-dark eyes were dreamy. 'Steve visiting Kyoto—come to my store to buy wedding present for friend in Tokyo. I advise him and we talk a little. He wait for me when store close and we go to cinema.' She dropped her eyes shyly. 'We fall in love—that is how Steve say it.'

Just like that, Sue thought. It takes no time at all, and the picture of Luke Masters came treacherously into her mind. She pushed it away impatiently. 'And you'll be married and live happily ever after,' she said.

Mariko's face changed. 'Very near we not marry at all,' she said, so low that Sue had to lean closer to hear. 'Very near I lose Steve. But Mr Masters save him. Mr Masters very brave and Steve think he wonderful. I too think he wonderful. You think so, yes?' She gave Sue a funny little upwards look.

Sue felt the heat in her cheeks. Had the quiet Mariko noticed something in the few moments they had all been together at the hospital? Had she been as obvious as that? 'Yes, I think so too,' she said. 'He is very good-looking.'

Mariko nodded wisely. 'Looks not always important,' she said. 'Shall we go now? I go to shop to have kimono . . .' She stopped with a puzzled frown and drew her hands over her slim body, in pantomime.

'Fitted?' Sue suggested.

'That is right—fitted. You come?'

'Of course. I'd love to see it.' As they emerged on to the crowded street Sue had a warm feeling that she and Mariko had begun to be friends.

The most satisfactory thing about the afternoon, Sue reminded herself at intervals, was that she was too interested in and fascinated by everything she saw to think very much about Luke Masters. Mariko's kimono for the wedding was a sumptuous affair of heavy white silk, held in round the waist by a sash—an *obi*, Mariko explained—exquisitely embroidered in red and turquoise, and hanging to the floor. The headdress she would wear was a traditional wide band of stiff, pale-pink silk. She held it to her head, but Sue gathered that it could only be fixed in place properly when Mariko was wearing the wig that would reproduce the high, formal style required for important, full-dress occasions. Sue was thinking that the whole outfit must have cost the earth and more, until Mariko explained in her funny broken English that all but the very richest of brides hire their wedding kimonos—they would cost far too much to buy.

After the fitting, Mariko took Sue round the shopping streets. They gazed at the glittering displays behind the plate-glass windows and wandered through two large department stores where everything seemed to Sue wildly expensive. Mariko proudly showed Sue the counter where she had worked and introduced Sue to the pretty young woman who had taken her job, and whose name was Akiko. On sale were a selection of souvenirs, 'To remember you of your visit,' Akiko explained painstakingly, and pointed to a tiny model ship made entirely of tortoise-shell. 'You like?'

'It's beautiful,' Sue sighed, picking up the little object, not more than an inch long. Suddenly her heart began to beat a little faster as the idea occurred to her: why not buy it to give to Luke as a thank-you present when they said goodbye? He had been kind to her and taken her around when really he hadn't needed to, she argued. And Japan was a great place for giving and receiving presents—he'd told her that himself. 'To remember you of your visit, and of a girl you met there,' she said to herself. 'How much does it cost?' she asked Akiko quickly, before she could change her mind.

As they left the store Mariko said with a small, concerned frown. 'Ship very expensive. You want to buy? Truly?'

Sue reassured her. 'Truly,' she said, her hand closing over the small parcel in the pocket of her blue suit.

Mariko smiled. 'We had better go to my home before you spend more money,' she said, and, remembering how much she had paid for the model ship Sue was inclined to agree. But she felt pleased and excited about her purchase and her resolution to forget all about Luke Masters had, for the moment at least, gone by the board.

Mariko's home was a bus-ride from the centre of Kyoto—a little wooden house with a curving tiled roof, and Mariko was quite obviously proud of her home. 'We live here for one year,' she told Sue. 'Before, we live always in a flat, high up.' She lifted an arm to the sky. 'Then my father retire and company sell him this nice house. Come in, please. My mother wish to know Steve's sister.'

As she got ready for bed, much later, Sue decided that the day had been a great success. In spite of the fact that Mariko's parents spoke only a few words of English they all seemed to have somehow managed to emerge understanding and liking each other. Mariko acted as interpreter and her parents smiled and nodded and Sue nodded back and admired everything: the neat little house with its one Western-style living room, crowded with ornaments and knick-knacks, the tiny garden with its rocks and bushes and a miniature shrine above an even more miniature pool.

Everything was pocket-size, including Mariko's two younger sisters of seven and eight, and the youngest of the family, the little boy, Minaru, who was obviously his mother's pride and joy. Sue was accustomed to the frictions of family life in Australia, and here the children seemed impossibly well-behaved and dis-ciplined, lining up in a row, like little soldiers, with their trousered legs and their buttoned tops, dropping to their knees and bowing to the floor to greet Sue, after which they entertained her with a well-rehearsed song, piping away in their high treble voices. Later the two girls produced pint-size violins and played a duet very competently.

'They're lovely, and so talented,' Sue said sincerely, and when Mariko had translated this remark for her parents the ice was well and truly broken. After that the evening went along swimmingly. Presents were given and admired and Sue found herself the possessor of several little boxes of sweets and biscuits. The evening meal, which they took in a nearby restaurant, lasted a long time and if Sue didn't exactly relish all the strange dishes that were put in front of her she managed to conceal the fact tactfully. At least she was beginning to enjoy the ever-present green tea very much.

Mariko was quite obviously pleased by the success of the visit and when Sue got into her taxi to return to her hotel, after much formal bowing and smiling and exchanging of thanks, Mariko whispered, 'Family all think you nice girl. That very good,' and Sue felt as if she had been tested and passed with honours.

It had all been a little exhausting though, and she couldn't help thinking how much easier her visit would have been if she had been accompanied by Steve. Or by Luke Masters. He crept inevitably into her mind as she sat in front of the mirror, brushing her hair and wondering how he had got on in Osaka, and if she would see him tomorrow morning. Perhaps, if he had already returned, he would come to her room and tell her of the day's events. It was still quite early, only just after ten o'clock. She shook her head impatiently and a cloud of silky hair swung round her face. 'Stupid,' she told her reflection aloud. 'Of course he won't come, why should he? And anyway, you decided not to think about him, didn't you?'

She slipped off her suit, got into the cotton kimono provided by the hotel, took a paper-back book from her travelling bag, and settled down to read until it was time to go to bed.

It was very quiet in the huge hotel, the lush carpets and furnishings muting all sound. After an hour Sue's pleasure at the success of her visit to Mariko's home was wearing off and she began to feel very alone. It was a little humiliating to be so utterly dependent on other people in this new and very strange land but she admitted frankly that it would be foolhardy in the extreme to go it alone. She wondered with a sigh what would happen tomorrow.

A tap at the door broke the silence, making her jump. 'Sue,' came Luke's voice. 'Are you asleep?'

She sped across the room and opened the door and at the sight of him standing there, his size nearly filling the doorway, she felt as if her heart stopped beating.

'You're back,' she said stupidly and she knew that her resolution not to think about him had been quite useless. He has been there all day, an overwhelming presence that filled all but the very front of her mind.

'I'm back,' he said, 'and very glad to get out of the rat-race atmosphere of Osaka. May I come in?'

He walked into the room without waiting for permission, and closed the door behind him.

Hastily Sue pulled out the one chair. 'Sit down,' she gabbled. 'I can sit on the bed. Would you like a drink, there are all sorts of bottles in my little fridge. Have you had dinner . . .' Something seemed to have happened to her throat and she choked on the last word.

He didn't seem to notice. He sank down wearily into

the chair and said, 'Would there be a Scotch by any chance?'

Sue fussed round getting the drink. When she turned to take it to him she saw that he was pulling off his tie and unfastening buttons so that his shirt fell open to show a mat of dark hair running down his chest. She stopped dead, gripped by an entirely new feeling low inside that sent a shudder through her. Her knees shook as she handed him the drink and moved away again quickly.

But her imagination had been working overtime. He merely tossed down the drink and lay back, stretching out his long legs before him. 'That's better. God, I'll be glad to get back home now. I'm getting very tired of endless conferences and buckets of *sake*. And Japanese business men always dress so correctly; they never take off their jackets even when the temperature is soaring, so of course one has to follow suit.' He grinned wryly at her. 'Don't take me too literally, I'm just whacked at the moment. Everything went very well, as a matter of fact, and that concludes my business in Japan.'

Sue sat on the edge of the bed and her heart seemed to have stopped beating again. 'You'll be flying back home tomorrow, then?' she said through stiff lips.

He frowned. 'Tomorrow? Lord, no. Whatever gave you that idea? I'm staying for the wedding, Steve will need my support. I hear he's being let out tomorrow afternoon so you and I will have to look after him and get him to the altar, or whatever they have here, on time. That's what I wanted a word with you about— then I'll take myself off to bed.' He yawned. 'How did your day go?'

Sue's heart seemed to have resumed its normal functioning. 'I enjoyed it very much,' she said primly.

'Good.' He didn't seem very interested. He sat up.

'Now, about tomorrow. 'I'll join you for breakfast and then we'll have the morning to see some of the Kyoto sights. You've really seen nothing yet and it'll be your last chance. We could get in one or two of the most impressive places before we call at the hospital for Steve to bring him back here. All right with you?'

'Yes,' gasped Sue, amazed by the way he organised her and everything else, 'but you really don't have to . . .'

He got to his feet. 'I don't really have to look after you,' he mimicked. 'You never learn, do you?' He was scribbling on the card that hung on the doorknob. 'Breakfast for two—sounds friendly, doesn't it?' He grinned. 'Be up good and early, little girl, we'll have a busy morning.'

He walked to the door. 'There's quite a few places I'd like to show you. And there's something I want to talk to you about, too. Something that might be important.' He smiled his enigmatic smile. 'Good night, little Sue.'

Sue sat transfixed when he had closed the door, her mind whirling. Then, as if suddenly powered by an inner force, she hurled herself across the room and flung open the door. She had to know what he meant by that extraordinary remark. She *had* to.

The long corridor was empty and silent. And she didn't even know the number of Luke's room.

She went slowly back inside and closed the door. The brute—making a remark like that and then just walking away. She'd like to . . . she'd like to . . . In sheer frustration she clenched her fists and pummelled the pillows on the bed. It didn't help much. She would have to wait until tomorrow, and she didn't know how she was going to get through the night.

CHAPTER FOUR

'I'VE booked a coach tour for us,' Luke announced as they finished breakfast next morning. 'I hope that's not too "touristy" for you. I thought it would be the best way for you to see some of the sights of Kyoto in the few hours we have to spare. Kyoto is bursting at the seams with shrines and temples and gardens and you'll only get the faintest flavour of all there is to see, but it'll be better than nothing. From what I gather the tour takes us round the main streets and then to Sanjusangen-do and to Ryoan-ji—that's the temple with the famous stone garden—and ends up with Kinkaku-ji—the Golden Pavilion. That sounds like enough for one morning. OK with you? Shall we get going then?'

He didn't wait for an answer and Sue stood up obediently, shrugging her arms into the jacket of her blue suit and wishing she had something more glamorous to wear. But you didn't argue when someone was offering to show you what you wanted to see, however brusque the offer.

There was more on her mind, however, than the sights of Kyoto or even the shortcomings of her wardrobe. All through breakfast she had hoped that Luke would enlighten her as to what it was that he wanted to talk to her about, but no, not a word. And if they were going on a coach tour there wouldn't be much opportunity for private conversation. She decided to tackle him here and now.

As she picked up her handbag she said with an attempt at casualness, 'What was it you wanted to say

to me specially? You mentioned something last
night . . .'

Luke's head jerked round and for the first time
she saw him look slightly disconcerted. 'Oh—that.
Yes. Well, there's no time now, we must be out by
nine o'clock. We'll have to wait for a better
opportunity.'

Which unsatisfactory statement only served to
increase Sue's curiosity. As she followed Luke out to
the lift she felt sure that she wouldn't be able to
concentrate on any of the wonderful sights of Kyoto.

But of course she did. The tour guide was a pretty
girl in a smart red uniform who stood up at the front
with a microphone, pointing out places of interest and
throwing in bits of history and information as the bus
rumbled through the main streets of the city. There
were, she told them thirteen hundred Buddhist
temples and four hundred Shinto shrines in Kyoto.
She smiled. 'Not possible to see all today.'

Luke, in the seat next to Sue's, leaned his head close
to hers. 'See what I mean?' he whispered. His mouth
was almost touching her ear; his lips brushed the
tendril of gold hair that strayed over it. She had put
her hair up into a knot this morning; it might, she
hoped, make her look older. Luke might not treat her
quite so obviously like a child on a school outing. She
nodded without speaking. If she turned her head ever
so slightly their lips would come dangerously close
and the thought made her tremble inside. She fixed a
tight little smile on her mouth and tried to listen to
what the guide was saying.

'We pass now Shinto shrine. Please to notice *torii* at
entrance. Two pillars at side and one across top.
Always *torii* at entance to Shinto shrine, most made of
wood. Old story say that bar across top was for
roosters to sit and sing in the morning so that Sun

Goddess would come out from dark cave and shine after night.'

'Charming,' mused Luke, close to Sue's ear. 'The *torii* looks a bit like a wooden Stonehenge—possibly dates from the same time, way back in antiquity.'

Sue nodded speechlessly. When he leaned towards her she was suffocatingly conscious of the way his arm and his thigh pressed against hers. Never before had she been so aware of her body and she was thankful for the noise of the coach's engine and the guide's monotonous staccato voice that must surely drown the racket her heart was putting up.

It was better when they got out of the coach and their party began to trail along behind the guide. Like all such conducted tours, there seemed far too much to take in all at once. The coach party was led into a great deep hall of a temple with massive wooden pillars that rose high up into the darkness beneath the roof. 'This is temple of one-thousand-and-one goddesses of mercy,' the guide intoned, and went into dates and names.

Sue's eyes were fixed on the forest of life-size gilded figures rising in tiers one above the other.'

'They look like petrified choirgirls,' she whispered to Luke. 'You almost expect them to burst into song. And how many arms have they got, for goodness sake?'

'Forty apiece,' he told her. 'Look at all those little ones sticking out of their backs.'

The heavy smell of incense and the peculiar gloomy atmosphere of the great hall was making Sue feel a bit hazy. 'Useful for housework. If you had forty hands you wouldn't need a kitchen robot, would you?' She started to giggle and had to stuff a handkerchief into her mouth.

The guide was still doling out names and dates and

going on about a famous samurai warrior who had
shot 13,053 arrows in one day. Luke put his arm
round Sue and steered her out into the open air.
'Behave yourself, infant,' he scolded, mock-severe.
'You'll get us thrown out of the party if you're not
careful.'

Sue made a face at him. It didn't seem to matter any
more if he treated her like a small child. After the
wedding tomorrow she would never see him again so
there wasn't any time left to correct the impression she
had made on him. Just for today she could relax and
enjoy the ecstasy of being with him. 'Sorry, sir.' She
pursed her lips up at him.

Outside the temple the sun shone full on her face
and Luke's own face was in shadow. So she nearly
passed out when he suddenly bent his head and kissed
her lips. 'Funny little Sue,' he said softly. 'I like you
very much.'

It was a horrible anti-climax when their party
emerged at that moment and they had to trail back to
the bus. As they took their seats again Sue felt as if
she were blushing all over. But Luke's sudden
impulse did not appear to have disturbed him in the
slightest. 'I think you'll enjoy Ryoan-ji more,' he
said conversationally. 'The stone gardens are out of
this world.'

You're out of this world, Sue thought besottedly,
appallingly aware of the strong, hard masculine form
beside her. She could no longer try to kid herself—she
was crazily in love with Luke Masters. She pushed
back a straying lock of hair with trembling hands.
'Stone gardens sound most unlikely,' she gabbled.
'Tell me about them, I'd rather hear it from you than
from our guide. You know a lot about Japan, don't
you? The way you trot out all the Japanese names is
most impressive. You must have visited here often.'

'I was here for three years, working for another firm,' he said. 'I fell in love with the place. It's a fascinating mixture of tradition and high-tech industry. Tourists think the old Japan is disappearing and they flock to see it before it sinks without trace. But not so—the Japanese value their ancient traditions too much to let them go. And I don't believe it's all in the interest of the tourist trade either, like some other Eastern places I could name. You wait until we get to Ryoan-ji and I think you'll see what I mean.'

Sue concentrated desperately on what he was saying, storing up and treasuring every word so that when he had finally gone she could remember this magic time together, when he was putting himself out to please her.

She had seen pictures of the Japanese stone gardens in her books, but the actuality was a totally different experience. The garden itself was a rectangle, about the size of a tennis court, and in it there were no paths, no trees, no flowers or foliage. Only a flat surface of gravelly sand, raked in precise silvery lines like a meticulously-mown lawn. In the sand were embedded weathered stones, only fifteen of them in the whole garden—Sue counted them—of different sizes and arranged in a seemingly erratic, but strangely satisfying way.

'We're lucky, it's not too crowded,' Luke said, leading Sue a little away from the main party. Even so, there were a great many people around the garden, sitting on the wooden steps of the temple building that overlooked it. Somehow Luke managed to make room for Sue and himself on the bottom step, almost at a level with the garden. 'It's supposed to be a better experience if you view it from ground level,' he whispered in her ear. Although there were so many people there there was no laughing or chattering—

very little noise altogether, mostly hushed voices and
the clicking of cameras. It was almost as if the garden
itself were exuding a kind of spiritual power.

Luke moved closer. 'Well, what do you think?'

'It's—wonderful,' Sue breathed. 'There's something
about it—I would never have dreamed...' She
stopped trying to find words for the effect this strange
place was having upon her. 'I'd like to come here
alone, in the moonlight,' she sighed at last.

He didn't laugh at her. 'I know what you mean,' he
said quietly, and after that they didn't speak again
until their party crowded back into the bus. Then
everyone began to talk at once.

'You really loved it, didn't you?' Luke said. 'That
must be the artist in you. You didn't go imagining
mountain peaks rising from the clouds, or islands
rising from the sea, or even a lunar landscape. That's
as far as most people get.' He glanced round the
chattering tourists in the other seats.

Sue felt as if he had pinned a medal on her chest. He
understood her a little and that was marvellous—it
made up for everything. 'My father would have loved
it too,' she said, and they didn't speak again until the
bus arrived at the next stopping place.

'We now at Kinkaku-ji, Golden Pavilion,' the guide
announced. 'Temple built in 1394 and burnt down by
mad monk in 1950. But since, temple rebuilt just as
before. Please be prepared for many Japanese tourists.
In Japan we like to visit our beautiful places.'

'Too true,' murmured Luke as they climbed out of
the bus. 'It's like Picadilly Circus.' His arm found its
way round Sue's waist as they mingled with the
crowds drifting along the tree-lined paths. There was
no temple to be seen. Then, suddenly, the path turned
a corner and Sue stopped, catching her breath. An
exquisitely fragile building cast the reflection of its

golden façade and balconies and tiers of uptilted pagoda roofs on to a lake, where the water was scattered with lotus plants. Pine trees rose from a tiny islet, and round the edges of the lake and behind everything loomed the outline of a mountain, rising up as if guarding this unique and delicate place of beauty.

It was a magic moment for Sue. Something she had read about and dreamed about had come to life before her eyes and she almost stopped breathing as she stood leaning on the wooden railings beside the lake in case it should disappear again. Luke's arm was still around her, although the crowd had passed on, and now his closeness seemed all part of the same delight. Her great blue eyes were misty as she raised them to his. 'I think it's the most beautiful thing I've ever seen,' she said.

He smiled down at her and in the dappled sunshine his eyes were darkly brilliant, his teeth creamy and regular against the bronzed skin. 'I'm inclined to agree,' he said, not taking his eyes from her face. 'I'm not sure if we're going to be led round inside. Do you want to go?'

'I'd much rather stay outside,' Sue said.

'My own sentiments exactly. I think this is where we detach ourselves from the mob and explore the gardens on our own.' He walked forward to where the guide had gathered her small flock around her. Sue could hear the sound of her voice trilling on and on. Then it stopped as Luke approached and spoke to her. Something changed hands and he turned back again.

'I told her we'd find our own way back,' he told Sue, rejoining her beside the wooden railings. 'Come on, let's try and find a quiet spot.'

He took her arm and they wandered off through the landscaped gardens, between the trees and shrubs, past little pavilions, over delicate bridges until they came to a wood. The crowds of people had thinned out here and at last there was nobody but their two selves.

Luke stopped. 'Let's sit down here,' he said. 'I want to talk to you.'

It was coming at last and he sounded oddly serious. Sue sat down beside him on the trunk of a fallen tree and waited, her heart beating unevenly. When she couldn't bear the silence any longer she rushed into speech.

'It's lovely here.' She looked around at the trees, touched by autumn reds and yellows, at the carpet of golden leaves beneath their feet. 'Peaceful.'

He glanced down at her and said, 'Peace—that's a strange thing for someone of your tender years to appreciate. Don't you ever yearn for discos and rock concerts?'

'Not particularly,' she said. 'Should I?'

He didn't answer that. He said, 'What a puzzle you are, Sue. In some ways you seem like a child still and in other ways surprisingly mature. Which leads me directly to what I wanted to say to you.'

This conversation was taking on an air of unreality. Sue leaned her palms on the rough bark of the tree, and waited.

'I've been thinking quite a lot about what you told me yesterday,' Luke spoke slowly, picking his words, 'and it occurs to me that possibly we could both do each other a good turn. Let me explain. I have a cottage in Cumbria, near Windermere. I also have a small son of nine-and-a-half who's at present a weekly boarder at a prep school in Ambleside. He comes back to the cottage each weekend and I do my best to be there, but sometimes it just isn't possible if I have to go abroad or if something urgent crops up in London. Then he has to put up with the housekeeper in residence and I find none of them stays very long. The old family retainer type of housekeeper exists mostly in novels, I imagine. I have nightmares about Christopher coming back one Friday night and finding the cottage empty. It would be a great weight off my mind to have someone there that I could trust.' His grey eyes searched her face. 'Are you getting the picture?'

Sue swallowed. She didn't know what she had expected, but certainly it wasn't this. 'I—don't quite know. Are you offering me a job as housekeeper?'

He smiled. 'Not precisely. You want to go back to England—particularly to the Lakes. I need someone to live there. It seems to fit in, although I admit we'd have to work out details. But—just for a start—how does the idea appeal?'

To live in Luke's house—to see him often—to care for his son—to get back to her beloved Lake District—Sue's mind went into a spin.

He was watching her face. 'What's the problem—I can see there is one. Are you thinking it would be too lonely? I have plenty of good neighbours and I'd make sure there was someone living in to do the housework and as much of the cooking as you didn't want to do. And if you're so partial to lakes I can offer you a lake too—my cottage overlooks Lake Windermere. I had the bright idea that you might like to take up your art training again. You wouldn't be far from Lancaster—only a short buzz down the motorway. Well, what do you think?'

She said weakly. 'You're a brilliant salesman, Mr Luke Masters. But you don't have to sell me that idea.'

'Marvellous. Then we can——'

'But I'm sorry,' Sue went on. 'It's all quite impossible.'

'Impossible? There's no such word.'

That was the successful business man talking. And of course this was a business proposition. 'There is for me,' she said.

'Tell me then and we'll iron it out.'

She shook her head, biting her lip. She thought of the endless dry stretches of Langeroo and she had a crazy notion that the devil himself was tempting her, showing her visions of lakes and fields and hills and rivers and the green of the grass and the soft rain on her face. She tried to hang on to reality. She mustn't spin impossible rainbow dreams that Luke would fall in love with her. She wasn't in Luke's league, and she must remember that he would bring women with him to his cottage, sophisticated women from his own world, who would look upon her as a superior servant.

If only she hadn't fallen in love with him! If only he had been twenty years older and a widower who played golf to keep his weight down, and dozed over the television in the evenings, then she would have been overjoyed to go back to England with him to be his housekeeper, to see her beloved Lakes again.

But Luke Masters—lean and dynamic and effort-lessly (and possibly unconsciously) oozing sex-appeal! She would live in dread that one day he would decide to marry again. Living in Luke's house would be condemning herself to a long torture. 'I just couldn't,' she said. 'Sorry.'

He sighed as if he were keeping his patience with an effort. 'I've made a suggestion that seems good to me. I think you might at least tell me why you're turning it down flat.'

She sat up straight. She had to think quickly now— he mustn't guess how desperately she was tempted. 'Well . . .' she spread out her hands, laughing a little, improvising. 'I'd have thought it was obvious. I couldn't just walk out on my people in Australia. They've been marvellous to me and I'm sure they've never dreamed that I wasn't completely happy with them. I couldn't just say, "I'm taking a housekeeper's job back in England so goodbye and it's been nice knowing you." They'd be horribly hurt.'

He said, 'You can't go through life without hurting anyone, you know. It can be as much a sin to be too unselfish as to be too selfish.'

'Yes, I've heard that argument,' she said. 'It's never quite convinced me.'

'If they love you so much, surely they'd want your happiness?' The quiet, understanding, companionable Luke of the stone garden had gone. He was irritable again, impatient, expecting her to fall in with his wishes.

Suddenly she turned on him. 'Oh, it's so easy for you. You're the kind of man who grabs just what he wants. I'm sure you can always find good reasons why you should have it.'

For a moment he looked taken aback, as if a fluffy kitten had suddenly reared up and spat at him. But immediately he regained his composure. 'But they would,' he insisted. 'They would want your happiness. Go on, admit it.'

He was edging her into a corner—that was the way business men functioned. 'OK, I admit it.' She was fighting him now; she had almost forgotten what the issue was. All she knew was that she had to convince him. She lifted her chin stubbornly. 'What I'm not prepared to do is to tell them that I'd be happier working in England as a—a sort of glorified housekeeper than staying in Australia as part of their family.'

'H'm.' He got to his feet and paced up and down, the leaves crunching under his feet. Then he stopped before her, arms folded, looking down. 'I have another suggestion to make that might solve all your difficulties. How about if you married me?'

'Very funny.' Sue wished he hadn't said that. It might be a joke to him but to her it was like a blow over the heart.

'I'm serious,' he said and she looked up with wide startled eyes and saw that he was.

'But—but . . .' she stammered.

He lowered himself down beside her again and took one of her hands, stroking it absently. 'Listen, Sue, it's not such a crazy idea as you might think. I daresay Steve has told you that my marriage has broken up. My wife and I were divorced just over six months ago after ten years of fairly constant in-fighting. I don't intend to risk repeating the performance so you won't expect romantic promises of undying love. That word simply doesn't exist for me any longer.' His eyes were suddenly bleak, but then almost immediately he was smiling at her encouragingly.

'Think about it,' he said. 'It may sound like only half a marriage, but it could work very well. Christopher is due to move on to his public school in about eighteen months or so and then this weekend difficulty won't arise. At that stage you and I could— reconsider our position.'

She looked straight at him. 'You mean—get a divorce?' This couldn't be happening; they couldn't be sitting here talking so calmly about marriage and divorce. It was all part of some fantastic dream.

'If you wanted it.' He was looking pleased with himself now as he enlarged on his idea. 'By then your course at art school would probably be coming to an end. It would seem a good point to decide exactly what you wanted to do with your life.' His mouth twitched wryly. 'I can't very well expect you to remain tied up to a disillusioned middle-aged man for good.'

'How old are you?' Sue said, asking the question to gain time.

'I'm thirty-six. I can give you sixteen years, but perhaps that would be all to the good.'

'Why?'

'Well . . .' once again he looked faintly taken aback '. . . I get the impression that you aren't very— experienced in the ways of this wicked world. Little Miss Innocence from the Outback,' he added teasingly.

'It isn't the Outback,' she said—as if it mattered! 'Well—not exactly.'

'All right, I take the Outback back, if you'll excuse the pun. I'll just say Little Miss Innocence. You are, aren't you?'

It was fantastic. What he was suggesting was vitally, earth-shakingly important—he was actually asking her to marry him—and yet he could treat it almost as a joke.

Sue drew a long, deep breath. 'You think I'm naïve and simple. You've been very kind to take me around with you and amuse me, as my brother isn't available, and I'm grateful. But you've quite obviously thought of me as a schoolgirl being taken out for a treat. And now, suddenly, you're asking me to marry you and take over some responsibility for your son. I really don't understand you at all, Mr Masters, and anyway, the answer is no. Definitely no.' Humiliatingly, after this show of independence, her voice stuck in her throat and she gulped.

He wasn't smiling now. He said, 'You prefer to go back to Australia?'

'Yes,' she said defensively.

'And marry Ross?'

Her heart sank like lead. 'I don't have to marry Ross if I don't want to.'

His dark eyebrows lifted. 'No?'

'No. I won't marry Ross, because I don't love him.' She didn't add that she hadn't arrived at that conclusion until this very moment.

'Ah—love again!' he sighed. 'There have been millions of good marriages that haven't been founded on romantic quicksands. I still think my suggestion is a good one. You couldn't have qualms about leaving your aunt and uncle if it were because you were going to get married. They'd understand that, wouldn't they? Well, think it over.'

He glanced at his watch and then took both her hands and pulled her to her feet. 'I suppose we'd better be getting back now if we're to get a bite of lunch and then pick up old Steve at the hospital. We've got his wedding to consider first—we can think about our own later.'

Walking beside him out of the cool of the gardens Sue's mind was in a white-hot turmoil. Luke was so matter-of-fact about his extraordinary proposal while she felt completely shattered. All she could think about clearly was that she hungered to hear him say, 'I love you.' Would he ever say that to her? If she married him she would be risking heartbreak, no doubt about that. Could she be content with what he called 'half a marriage'? The questions jostled each other round her brain and there was no answer to any of them.

'This calls for a celebration,' Steve said, easing himself on to the bed and carefully adjusting his arm, which was encased in plaster and hitched up in a sling. 'How about drinks all round?'

'Brilliant idea.' Luke strode across to the house telephone.

They were all back at the hotel—Steve and Mariko, Luke and Sue, and an atmosphere of pre-wedding excitement pervaded the hotel bedroom. Steve had taken possession of his own room and Sue had moved her things to another room two floors above. Luke had done marvels of organisation, it seemed to her: interviewing doctors and specialists; getting notes and prescriptions for Steve to take back to Tokyo with him; procuring taxis and transporting Steve with the minimum of discomfort; arranging for her to switch rooms; in short, taking charge of the proceedings in a characteristically masterful fashion.

Watching him, Sue was constantly reminded that he was a man who got what he wanted, and that one of the things he wanted just now was—her services. He had evidently decided that if he got her installed as his wife in his cottage in the Lake District she would have to stay and do her master's bidding. What sort of a marriage was that?

And yet—and yet—how marvellous it would be to be back in Windermere, to be there with him, even if it were only a marriage of convenience. The devil hadn't given up yet.

A waiter arrived with the drinks that Luke had ordered—Sapporo beer for the men and green tea for the girls with little bowls of biscuits, and the room began to take on a festive air. Mariko, flushed and pretty in her jeans and striped top, sat on the bed beside Steve and held his beer glass and fed him biscuits. 'Like geishas,' she said mischievously.

'But this is something you aren't allowed to do to geishas,' Steve grinned as he leaned over and kissed her lingeringly.

Luke perched on the arm of Sue's chair and put a

hand possessively on her shoulder. 'Before everyone gets too carried away I've got an announcement to make,' he said.

Sue stiffened. Surely he wasn't going to . . .

But he went on, 'I've been on the 'phone to the Chairman in London to put him in the picture and he sends commiserations about the accident, Steve. Also congratulations on your marriage. But—on a different matter—he asks me to tell you that he's been looking through your files and he's very pleased with the way you've handled the job out here. He's decided to give you a step-up in the company, which will mean returning to London Office as from the beginning of next year. How do you feel about that?'

There was a silence in the room. Steve looked stunned. Then his mouth began to stretch into a wide smile. 'Well!' he said at last. He turned to his bride-to-be. 'How do *you* feel about it, my love?'

Mariko's pretty face was pink with delight. 'Oh yes, Steve, I like to live in London with you. Will be wonderful.'

'That settles it then.' Steve nodded to Luke. He was managing to keep his composure but Sue knew him well enough to see that he was, in his quiet way, quite overcome with pleasure. 'We'll be very happy to move back to the UK.'

Then he turned to Sue, his face suddenly rueful. 'But that means that we'll be even further apart than ever, Sis. That's a bad show.'

'Not necessarily,' Luke put in calmly, helping himself to a biscuit. 'I've had a bright idea that I've put to Sue. But perhaps she'd better tell you herself.' He gave her shoulder a little squeeze.

She looked up at him, utterly astounded. He was smiling smugly down at her, so sure he was going to get his own way, so pleased with himself for taking her by surprise like this. She felt a sudden strong surge of resistance. What he had done was more than cutting the ground from under her feet—it was very close to blackmail. Had he even spoken to his Chairman, or was this part of a plan to make sure she fell in with his wishes? She wouldn't put it past him. He'd no doubt been surprised and annoyed when she hadn't jumped at his proposal of marriage. If she now accepted weakly it would be confirming him in his assessment of her as a sweet, biddable little girl. She'd be stuck with that image in his eyes—probably for good. But to deny it all, to put him out of her life for good! She couldn't do it.

It took a split second for all this to pass through Sue's mind. Another split second to make her decision.

She got to her feet, shaking Luke's hand from her shoulder, and stood with her back to the window. They were all looking at her—Steve puzzled, Mariko with her usual composed little smile, Luke with a self-satisfied gleam in his eye. She turned to Steve, speaking directly to him. 'This will be a surprise to you, Steve, but I hope you'll understand and approve. The fact is that Luke has a cottage in the Lake District and he needs someone reliable to be there when his son Christopher comes home from school for weekends. He's offered me the job of housekeeper and the temptation to go back to the Lakes has been too much for me so I've accepted.'

She glanced at Luke. The smile had disappeared from his face, his lips were compressed grimly. She felt a small spurt of something like triumph. At least she had surprised him; he must have been so sure she would jump at the opportunity of marrying him.

Steve was staring at her doubtfully. 'Well—I don't know—this needs thinking about.'

Luke walked over to the tray and poured himself some more beer. 'I know what you're thinking, pal, but I assure you my intentions are strictly honourable. For the record, I asked Sue to marry me—so that the proprieties should be observed, but she has obviously decided that I'm not a very good marriage risk—and I can't say I altogether blame her,' he added, tossing down his drink.

He gave Sue a baleful look and she saw that he was angry as well as surprised. She met his eyes coolly. 'Marriages of convenience are a bit out of date, surely? Anyway, as you say, the idea doesn't appeal to me. But . . .' she turned back to Steve '. . . but I do yearn so terribly to go back home, Steve. Aunt Meg and Uncle Ray have been very kind to me and I'm fond of them both but the prospect of seeing the lakes and the mountains again is just too much for me. You love it there yourself, I'm sure you know how I feel. Just say you understand and that you'll help me to explain to the folk in Langeroo, there's a darling.'

Steve seemed mollified. He turned to Mariko who was smiling rather blankly. She probably hadn't understood very much of what they had been saying. 'Sue is going back to England with Luke,' he explained. 'He's offered her a job.'

Mariko clapped her little hands and her dark eyes danced. 'That is good. Some time we will meet with each other in UK and we will all be happy, yes?'

'Yes,' Sue said. 'We'll all be happy.' She couldn't look at Luke. 'Now, Steve, could we ring them in Australia, do you think, and explain?'

The next few minutes were difficult. Aunt Meggie was first astounded, then a little tearful. 'Oh dear, this is a shock, we shall all miss you so much. And what will Ross think about it? How long is the job for, and will you be coming back soon?'

When Sue began to get a little incoherent, Steve took the 'phone from her and after he had talked quietly and sensibly for a time Sue could hear Auntie Meg's voice become more resigned. He handed the 'phone back to Sue finally.

'Dear Auntie Meg, please don't be cross with me, I love you both very much and I can never thank you enough for taking me in when you did. I'll come back and see you soon if you'll have me. It's just that—that I've got this longing to see my old home again—and then this offer came up—and I couldn't say no. Give my love to Uncle Ray and the boys . . . and to Ross.' She bit her lip, trying to steady her voice. 'It wouldn't have done, you know—Ross and me. He's a fine man but I don't love him, so I couldn't—ever . . . I'll write you a long letter as soon as we get back to England. I promise.' She put down the receiver, her eyes glinting with tears.

Luke had apparently been studying his notebook during the telephone conversation. Now he tucked it back into his pocket. 'Well, the next item on the agenda is to organise Steve's gear for his wedding tomorrow. You'll have to leave that to me, my lad, I'll get round to the hiring place straight away. We're about the same height, and I can judge your size. Now you rest yourself, I'm sure Mariko will look after you. Sue and I will take ourselves off for a while.'

Sue's arm was gripped firmly and she was propelled towards the door. When they reached the lift Luke released her and stood with his back to the gates, barring her way in. 'Why, you little twister!' His tone was accusing his eyes were hard.

'What do you mean?' She met his gaze a little defiantly, but it was with an effort. She had challenged him and she thought she had won, but he looked a very formidable man, towering there before her.

'You know damn well what I mean. I wasn't talking about giving you a housekeeper's job. I seem to remember asking you to marry me.'

'Oh—that!' She flicked it away casually. 'You didn't really want to marry me—that was an afterthought. You wanted a reliable housekeeper and you've got yourself one. I can cook pretty well and I promise I won't leave you in the lurch. Anyway, once I get back to Windermere I certainly shan't want to live anywhere else.'

He stuck his hands in his pockets, leaning against the lift gate. 'For the record, what made you change your mind? What about all that guff about not wanting to hurt your relatives in Australia?'

He was so smug. She wanted to hit that superior smile off his face. 'I decided to take your advice,' she said coolly. 'To the effect that if you want something enough you have to risk hurting people to get it.'

'H'm.' He surveyed her through half-closed eyes. 'You really are a surprising little creature. You want to see your beloved lakes as much as that?'

'Yes, oh yes, of course I do, I simply can't wait to get back,' she babbled. Once, not long ago, that would have been the whole truth. Now it was only a very small part of it.

'And you're sure you wouldn't like to marry me? It would make things simpler.'

'Quite sure, thank you.' It wouldn't make things simpler—it would make them more difficult. 'For one thing I wouldn't marry unless I was in love. And anyway, the whole idea is quite absurd. We hardly know each other.'

His dark brows lifted. 'We know each other as well as most people who marry do. And may I remind you that we've already shared a bed?'

Her cheeks flamed. 'Oh you—you——' She glared at him helplessly.

She stepped round him and pressed the lift button. 'I'll go up to my room,' she said. 'I want to put my things away and get my dress pressed for the wedding tomorrow.'

'Ah yes, of course.' The lift arrived and he opened the gates and stood aside with a mocking little bow. 'It's all yours, my lady. We lesser mortals will walk down.' As the lift bore her upwards she had a fleeting glimpse of his tall, straight back disappearing down the corridor.

She reached her room a little breathless. That had been an odd little fight and she wasn't quite sure who had won.

But at least she had made her own decision and stuck to it and when she sat down in front of her mirror, she saw that her eyes were shining bluer than ever before.

Was it, perhaps, the light of battle?

CHAPTER FIVE

SUE had resisted Steve's suggestion that she should hire a kimono to wear at the wedding. Next morning, as she slipped into her simple light-wool dress in a pale celery-green she was confident that it suited her, and she felt it matched her new-found image. She spent ages over her hair, twisting it into a heavy, silver-gilt coil, and even more ages on her make-up. At Langeroo she seldom used any make-up at all, but she had taken care to read up on the magazines before she left and buy in a modest supply of cosmetics on her last visit to the small town twenty miles away.

When she finished making the best of herself she looked in the mirror, satisfied with what she saw there—a cool, attractive young woman; certainly not the child that Luke had seen her until now.

She stared at her reflection, suddenly appalled. She was getting dressed for Steve's wedding, Steve who cared about her, Steve her beloved brother. And all the time she was thinking of Luke, and the impression she would make on him. Luke, who only wanted to use her for his own convenience.

Feeling guilty and ashamed she jumped up and ran out to the lift to wait downstairs for the two men.

It had rained in the night but today Kyoto had put on its loveliest face for the wedding of Steve and Mariko. As Sue got out of the car with Luke and Steve and walked under the great vermilion *torii* to the Shinto shrine, the autumn sun shone down brilliantly, turning the leaves to gold and the grey-tiled roof of the shrine to silver.

The wedding ceremony itself was too strange for her to experience it directly; she had to remind herself that that was Steve, her brother, standing there beside Mariko—wearing the very wide, striped trousers, the short black kimono with one sleeve hanging loose to accommodate the damaged arm in its sling. Seen from the back, only his neatly-brushed light brown hair was familiar and the way his ears stuck out a little. That made her throat contract with tenderness. Dear Steve, he was such a darling, he deserved happiness. And she believed he would find it with the gentle Mariko.

Mariko, serious and composed, was a floating vision in her kimono of stiff white brocade, the wide *obi* circling her ridiculously small waist and hanging to the ground; the broad band of silk arranged round the dark wig, which was piled high in traditional style, her face made-up to creamy perfection, smooth as a pearl. Sue could well believe that it had taken the hired dresser two hours or more this morning to produce this picture of serene beauty.

She watched the robed priest and his helpers, one of them a young woman, going through the unintelligible ceremony. At one point the priest raised his arms and pirouetted in a kind of solemn dance. It was all so different from a wedding in a village church at home—different and yet the same. A man and a woman pledging themselves in love for each other and hope for the future. Sue turned her head a fraction and glanced at Luke, on the row behind her. He was staring straight ahead, his face expressionless. Was he remembering his own wedding that had gone so wrong?

Her heart squeezed up with love and pity, because a broken marriage seemed such a waste, but she reminded herself that he wouldn't want either. He'd ruled love out of his life and he wasn't the kind of man

who would welcome pity. Probably he wasn't
remembering his own wedding at all; more likely he
was working out the terms of his next business
contract. He was a hard man, cynical, tough, and she'd
better keep that in mind. She went cold as she
wondered if she had made a terrible mistake in
promising to return to England with him. The future
seemed shrouded in doubt.

As the wedding pursued its ritualistic course to the
end Sue tried to think of Steve and Mariko and how
good it was that they would be coming to England in
the New Year. *If things go wrong,* she thought with
relief, *I shall have Steve to turn to,* and then, with self-
disgust, *Grow up, Sue, you've made your decision, so
stick to it.*

At last the ceremony was over. The sound of the
reedy, twangy Japanese instruments, with the occasional percussion thump, died away. Afterwards there
were formal, stiff group photographs taken on the
veranda of the shrine. The little photographer bustled
about, arranging and rearranging everyone, fussing
with the hang of the womens' kimonos, the exact way
the mens' hands rested on their knees, the angle of the
childrens' dark heads.

Afterwards, the party gathered in a large hall behind
the shrine for the wedding feast. Sue found herself
seated at the long top table between Steve and an
elderly gentleman with a white beard, whom she
gathered was one of Mariko's relatives.

Steve leaned towards her. 'How goes it, Sis? Getting
on OK? Not too baffled by everything?' He lowered
his voice. 'I'm feeling a bit out of my depth myself, in
spite of the fact that I've been coached.'

'I'm loving every minute.' Sue smiled brilliantly. 'I
just wish I could understand what everyone is saying.'
She looked round the room, which was almost filled

by its four long tables, arranged in a square formation, with a kind of empty well in the centre. Luke was sitting at the left-hand table next to a pretty Japanese girl in a black kimono. He was leaning towards her, talking and smiling. Sue looked away again quickly. 'What a lot of guests! And Mariko looks absolutely out of this world.' Her own voice sounded odd in her ears as she chattered on, but Steve didn't appear to notice anything unusual.

'Doesn't she just? Poor darling, she can hardly breathe in her outfit—we're due to retire in a few minutes for a costume change.'

There were speeches which Sue, of course, couldn't understand. Then Steve and Mariko disappeared and the guests, who had behaved very properly at first, began to loosen up as the drink flowed. Sue picked at the contents of the little bowls on the small tray in front of her and drank the *sake* in her cup. She smiled vaguely at the elderly gentleman beside her and they nodded to each other amiably, but all the time she was almost painfully aware of Luke. Once she caught his eye and waited for him to smile, but he just turned back to continue his conversation with the girl in the black kimono. Oh God, she thought dolefully, I love him so much and what am I going to do about it? I'm laying up a pile of trouble for myself, going back to England with him. But she couldn't have returned tamely to Australia and her old life—not when she had a chance to be near Luke.

Steve and Mariko returned, Mariko looked even more ravishing in the flowery brightness of the kimono she was wearing now. She had discarded the stiff silk headdress and a single red rosebud was tucked into her high-piled dark wig. She was carrying a gaily-coloured paper parasol covering them both, and they each held a lighted taper. Slowly progressing round the tables they set light to candles that sprouted from lacquered holders, until little lights glowed everywhere, falling softly on the yellow and scarlet of the flower arrangements.

The feast went on for ages; the speeches seemed interminable. Presents were showered upon the happy couple and Sue was delighted that they seemed pleased with her own modest offering of table mats that she had designed and embroidered herself, and a little framed water-colour of their cottage in the English Lake District that her father had painted. She had taken two of his pictures with her to Australia and now, she had decided, Steve should have one of them. Steve squeezed her hand hard as he thanked her and she knew how much he appreciated the thought and the gift.

All the guests had presents too—small boxes covered with rough-textured silk material and tied with a kind of fuzzy ribbon in a bright pink colour, were placed beside each tray and soon all the tables were overflowing with a tide of pink ribbon.

Then a black-robed musician sat cross-legged in the central well between the tables and played traditional Japanese music. Sue's head was beginning to ache and Steve kept filling up her cup with *sake*. He was obviously enjoying all this tremendously. He even made a little speech in Japanese. He'd changed, Sue thought, from the quiet, serious Steve she remembered. That's what being in love does for you.

Suddenly her heart missed a beat. Someone was standing behind her and she knew without looking round that it was Luke. 'Sorry to break up the party but we've got a train to catch. We'd better be getting back to the hotel, Sue.' He touched Steve's shoulder. 'How about it, you two? Shall we meet up in Tokyo tomorrow?'

It had been arranged that Steve and Mariko should go back to Steve's apartment in Tokyo after the wedding. Later, when Steve had been finally dismissed by the hospital, they would have a honeymoon in Kyushu. Luke had managed to book a seat for Sue on his flight back to England the following day. Tonight they would put up at the hotel in Tokyo where Luke had taken Sue when she arrived from Australia. She had listened vaguely when all this was being planned, not really taking it in. Everything, at the moment, had a dreamlike quality about it. Not until she finally arrived at Luke's cottage by the lake would she be able to believe that it was all true.

The future stretched in front of her, beckoning, frightening. But at least she had made her decision and she had made it alone. She had decided to take the risk.

It was cold and raining when the plane got into Heathrow and as the sleety rain lashed the window of the taxi that was taking them to Luke's London apartment Sue felt frozen, inside and out. The long plane journey had seemed endless. Luke had retreated into a silent world of his own, and beyond attending briefly to her need for food and drink, had hardly spoken a word, all those hours. Sue had tried to sleep but she was too tense to do more than nod off for a quarter of an hour or so now and again, to wake with a jump, her limbs stiff, her head full of dismal thoughts. Luke was obviously bored with her; he had acted on impulse and now he was regretting it; he'd found that he'd made a mistake in taking a young, inexperienced girl back to England with him and was wondering how he could decently get out of the situation. When the plane touched down for its stop at Anchorage they got out and walked about, but the sight of the famous stuffed polar bear did nothing to raise her spirits.

Luke's flat was a luxury bachelor apartment. Sue didn't take in its exact whereabouts, but by then she wasn't taking in very much of anything.

'We'll kip down for a couple of hours before we leave for the north,' Luke said, pulling off his tie. 'Chris should be getting home about six and I'd like to be there before him to give him a surprise. I'll put a call through to Mrs Benson before we leave to say we're on our way and she can get a meal going for us.'

'You're driving up?' Sue asked.

He nodded. 'Any objections? I promise you I shall be quite safe on the road, the jet-lag won't set in until later.' He glanced at her briefly, his voice curt.

'I didn't mean . . .' Sue began. Oh, what was the use? He wasn't listening to her.

'You can have the bed and I'll doss down here.' He opened the door of the bedroom and switched on the light, yawning as he did so. 'Bathroom's through there—look after yourself.' And that was how it was going to be from now on. She would be looking after herself. Gone was the man who had strolled by her side in the temple gardens, who had stood with his arm around her as they gazed over the lake beside the Golden Pavilion. She had chosen to be his house-keeper, his employee, and so long as she did her job he would take very little further interest in her. Somehow she must learn to put up with it.

At least, she tried to comfort herself as she drew the duvet up to her nose and snuggled into the bed where Luke had slept, at least she would be going home to the Lakes.

It seemed only a few minutes later that the light was switched full on and Luke was shaking her arm. She sat up, blinking. 'We've got to make a start now—straight away.' He shot the words at her. 'I've been trying to get through to Mrs Benson at home and there's no reply. We must get up there as quickly as we can.' His face was heavily shadowed; he looked desperately worried. 'I've been afraid of something like this,' he muttered, turning back to the living room.

Sue leapt out of bed and pulled on her skirt and jacket. Ten minutes later they were heading for the motorway in the big, glossy car that Luke had left parked in the underground garage of the apartment. The afternoon traffic in London was heavy and he drove with furious concentration as Sue sank into the depths of the soft leather passenger seat and stopped herself from asking questions.

But when they reached the motorway she couldn't keep silence any longer. 'What do you think might have happened?' she said, glancing up at Luke's stern profile outlined against the rain-dark afternoon sky outside.

'I don't think, I'm bloody sure,' he barked, not taking his eyes from the wet road. 'The Benson woman has done a bunk. I wasn't too happy about her but she came with good references a couple of months ago. They're all the same—get bored, with no bingo and no neighbourhood gossip.'

'And Christopher is due to come home today? How does he get home?'

'Does it matter?' he growled.

'Yes, I think it does. If I'm going to take charge I need to know.'

He changed to the fast lane and overtook three cars before he said, 'Fred from the local garage picks him up at school on Friday afternoons and takes him back on Monday mornings.'

'And what would Christopher do if he found the house empty?'

'Use your imagination, girl, your guess is as good as mine,' he snapped. 'What would you have done at nine years old if you got back to a cold, empty house miles from anywhere, on a wet November afternoon?'

'Yes,' said Sue, feeling crushed. 'I see what you mean.' She didn't ask any more questions and Luke drove on—and on—and on . . .

Once they stopped at a motorway service station and drank black coffee, standing up in tense silence, and then they were on their way again. Some time after that the rain changed to snow and soon there was a powdering covering the roadside verges. Sue glanced at the big clock on the dashboard, which said twenty to six. It was quite dark now and Luke was driving more carefully as the snow gathered on the windscreen and the wipers squeaked and groaned, brushing it aside. 'How much further?' Sue asked.

'Thirty miles. Forty.' A pause. 'Not a very good welcome for you, is it? Sorry you came?'

'No.' In November in Langeroo the sun would be rising on another hot, cloudless summer day. But she was here and Luke was beside her. She was in love and where he was she wanted to be. It was as simple, or as complicated, as that.

It wasn't long before they left the motorway. The snow lay thicker on the deserted country roads. The powerful headlights pierced black tunnels where trees overhung the road and once Sue caught a gleam of water to her right. Windermere, she thought, and she remembered the lake in Japan and how the sight of it had started all this. It seemed like another life.

'God!' She heard Luke's muttered exclamation as he brought the car to a halt and switched off the engine.

Sue saw the shadowy form of a low white house rising out of a thin covering of snow.

Luke was out of the car in a flash and had the front door open. Sue waited for lights to come on inside the house. They didn't.

She remembered only too well how the power had sometimes failed in their cottage, not far from here. It was a hazard of living in the deep countryside in the winter. She climbed stiffly out of the car and followed Luke into the house.

It was pitch dark inside, and very cold—clammy cold as if there had been no heat on for some time. She heard Luke blundering about, cursing and knocking into furniture and she waited. 'Christopher!' he bawled. 'Chris! Are you here?'

From somewhere above, the light of a torch appeared on a stairway. Sue looked up and saw the form of a little boy standing at the top of the stairs, wrapped in a blanket, peering down. 'Is that you, Dad? Gosh, am I glad to see you. It's jolly parky in here and Mrs Benson's hopped it and the juice has gone off.' Christopher hurled himself down the stairs, tripping over the blanket, and landed in Luke's arms.

Luke hugged him tightly, and the torch fell to the floor. Then Christopher must have caught sight of Sue, standing in the shadows by the door. 'Mummy,' he squealed joyfully. 'Mummy—you've come back.' He launched himself on her, his arms flung round her waist, his face pressed against her jacket, gibbering with excitement.

Sue stood transfixed, utterly at a loss what to do or say. Then, almost as if it chose the right dramatic moment, the power came on again and the hall was suddenly flooded with light.

Christopher loosened his hold, drawing back, his face a study of shock and disappointment. Luke stepped forward and put an arm round his son. 'This is Sue, Chris,' he said. 'She's going to live here and look after things.' He glanced at Sue and murmured, 'An understandable mistake—the hair's the same colour.'

'Hullo, Christopher.' Sue held out her hand, smiling. She judged that this wasn't the moment to trot out platitudes about hoping they would be friends. 'I expect you're hungry, aren't you?'

Christopher turned his back and walked towards the stairs. 'No,' he said. Sue guessed that there were tears in his eyes that he would rather have died than admit to.

Luke moved forward, his face stern, 'Christopher!' he barked.

Christopher stopped, still with his back to them.

'Shake hands with Sue and say hullo properly.'

'Hullo,' muttered Christopher. He turned round grudgingly and touched her outstretched hand without raising his head. Then he grabbed his blanket and stumbled up the stairs.

That little incident was best ignored. Sue said, 'Will you show me the kitchen, please. And will the heat come on? It's very cold in here.'

'Quite the efficient housekeeper, aren't you?' For a moment Luke glared darkly at her, and her inside quailed. Then he said, 'I'll cope with the boiler.' He led the way down a passage into a modern kitchen.

Propped up on the sink-unit was a piece of paper with spidery writing on it. Luke glanced at it and handed it to Sue.

'Dear Sir,' she read. 'I am sorry but I must leave to see to my sister's husband who has been took ill very sudden. I am sorry not to let you know but I have not got any address. The money is all right as I have been paid for this month. Yours faithfully, Mrs M. Benson.'

Sue handed the note back to Luke who opened the waste bin and dropped it in with a grimace of distaste. Then he went over to the boiler in the corner of the kitchen and started twiddling the knobs. 'We could be out of oil if something's gone wrong with the bloody delivery. That would put the finishing touch to a perfect homecoming,' he said savagely.

Sue was moving round the kitchen, looking in the fridge, opening cupboard doors, lifting the lid off the freezer to peer into its depths. 'There's plenty of food anyway,' she said. 'And couldn't you light a fire?' she added in a practical voice.

Muttering to himself Luke disappeared through a door into what looked like a scullery and emerged with a bucket of coal and a pack of newspaper.

'Does Christopher have any favourites for supper?' Sue asked.

Luke put down the bucket. 'He doesn't damn well deserve any supper, surly young brute.'

'How about egg and chips? Most kids like that and there are some of those oven chips in the freezer. I could soon do them under the grill.'

He picked up the bucket again. 'You're the cook,' he said ungraciously and went out of the kitchen.

Sue pulled a face at his retreating back and opened the freezer. Not so long ago she had felt desperately tired and rather depressed. It was wonderful how an emergency could put new energy into you. She switched on the electric grill and took eggs from the fridge. In ten minutes the frozen chips were sizzling under the grill.

Luke came in with a portable electric fire, plugged it in and switched on. 'I've got a fire going in the study,' he said, sounding a little less irritable. 'We can eat here. What would you like to drink? Something warming, I think. He went out again and came back with two bottles. 'Brandy or ginger wine?'

'Ginger wine, please. I love it.' He poured her a drink and helped himself from the other bottle. Then he sat down by the table and watched her as she turned the chips in the grill pan and started to fry the eggs.

'That's it,' she said, tipping the eggs on to plates, 'I'm jolly hungry, aren't you? I'll go and tell Christopher. Which is his room?'

Luke stood up, clattering back his chair impatiently. 'I'll go.'

Sue put a hand on his arm. 'Please let me,' she said quietly.

He looked down at her for a moment in silence. Then he shrugged. 'It's the second room to the left at the top of the stairs.'

She ran up the stairs and knocked briskly at the bedroom door. There was no answer so she opened it and put her head round. Christopher was sitting on the bed, wrapped in the blanket, a transistor thumping away beside him. Sue listened for a moment. 'Ah, that's Barney Helper, isn't it? He's good.' It was a shot in the dark but Sue had been well educated in the pop scene by her young cousins in Langeroo.

Christopher stared at her. He was a good-looking boy—or would have been if his mouth had been less sulky. Dark hair, dark eyes, ridiculously long lashes; he was a younger, more vulnerable edition of his father.

'There's supper on downstairs,' she said cheerfully. 'Egg and chips.' She had left the kitchen door open on purpose and now a mouth-watering smell drifted into the room.

Christopher still said nothing.

'Hurry up and come down before we eat them all.'

Sue glanced at the pile of books on the bed. So Christopher was a bookworm, like herself. That might break the ice between them, she thought hopefully as she went downstairs again.

By the time the eggs and chips were served out Christopher had appeared in the kitchen; he had brushed his hair and left the blanket behind.

'That's more like it,' grunted Luke as Christopher climbed on to a high stool beside him at the breakfast bar. 'Well, how was school this week?'

'All right,' mumbled Christopher, his mouth full of chips. Luke turned to Sue. 'My son, as well as being in the gymnastics team, seems to have developed a taste for art,' he said. 'You might get together on that.'

'Perhaps,' Sue said warily. She knew better than to rush into enthusiastic overtures of friendship with Christopher. 'Would you like some more chips, Mr Masters?'

Luke grinned at her. Like his son he was slowly thawing out. 'Sure would, Miss Larkin,' he drawled. 'That'd be jake.'

Sue went over to the cooker. 'Are you reminding me I ought to be back in Langeroo?' she said lightly.

'I'm glad you're not if this meal is a sample of your expertise,' he said. 'What have you been doing out there all these years since you left England?'

'Doing? There's never any problem in finding something to do at a farm. Cooking, cleaning, mending, looking after the chickens. And two young cousins to help my aunt cope with.'

'Ah.' Luke nodded sagely. 'I thought I detected an expert hand at work.' He glanced meaningfully at Christopher, who was tucking into his egg and chips, apparently taking no interest in the conversation.

Sue pretended not to understand. She had first-hand knowledge of just how much children took in of adults' conversation and she badly wanted to get off on the right foot with Luke's son.

'You didn't get much time to draw, or paint, or whatever you do?' Luke returned to his original question. Sue shook her head. That was a sore point that she didn't want to discuss.

'Then we must see you *do* get time here,' Luke went on smoothly. 'Now I've got you here I intend to give you every incentive to stay. I suggest you make contact with your old college fairly soon and see if you can enrol in a course for after Christmas. You can drive?'

Sue pulled a face. 'Anything on four wheels. Including a tractor.'

'I'm afraid we can't offer you a tractor, but there's an M.G. Metro in the garage. I'll get it going for you tomorrow. You'd better go into Windermere on Monday and see if you can find a woman to help you in the house. Obviously you know the district so I don't have to brief you on shopping or anything. You can open accounts at my bank—you'll probably like to keep the housekeeping separate from your personal account. I'll give you a cheque to be going on with. I think that about covers all the practical items. I'll have to get back to London tomorrow evening, and Chris will be going back to school on Monday morning so you'll be on your own. You'll be OK?' he added, and she thought she detected a note of concern in his voice but she might have been mistaken.

'Of course,' she said quietly.

All very neat and businesslike, Sue thought. I'm the housekeeper and I mustn't forget it. He had evidently decided by now that she was going to be useful to him and he'd do everything he could to make her comfortable; she mustn't read anything more into his thoughtfulness for her, his apparent interest in her taking up her art again.

He put down his table napkin with a satisfied grunt. 'That was good. Now I suggest we move into the study to have our coffee and see how my fire is burning up. Coming, Chris?'

Christopher shook his head. 'I'll go to bed,' he said. 'I want to read.'

His father shrugged. 'Please yourself. Good night then.' He certainly wasn't a very demonstrative parent.

'Good night.' Christopher glanced in Sue's direction and quickly away again. She smiled. 'Good night, Christopher.'

The study was a cosy little room. The light from a shaded table lamp fell on a roll-top desk, a side table and two big leather chairs. A fire was burning brightly in the grate and Luke threw a couple of logs on it as Sue poured out coffee. They took the chairs, one each side of the fire. Quite a domestic little scene, Sue thought and wondered how it would have been if she had agreed to marry him. Torment, hell, because she would have been longing for him to make love to her, hungry for him, dismally disappointed in the 'half-marriage' he had offered. No, it was far better like this, when he needn't even pretend to want her.

Luke leaned back, sipping his coffee, a brandy glass on the hearth beside him. 'It hasn't been much of a homecoming for you,' he said. 'It was no doubt childish of me but I rather wanted it to be—well, everything you expected.'

'I'm not disappointed,' Sue said sturdily. 'I've seen the Lakes in this mood many a time. A bit of snow won't frighten me away, if that's what you're thinking.'

He was silent for a long moment, then he said slowly, 'It wasn't—quite—what I was thinking.'

'No?' She sensed a change in him. His voice had softened, lost its abruptness.

'No,' he shook his head, smiling at her. 'I was thinking how lovely you look, Sue, sitting there with the firelight turning your hair to pure gold.' He smiled at her and his voice dropped huskily. 'Lovely, and very desirable.'

Sue's mouth fell open a little and her stomach seemed to disappear altogether.

He leaned forward and pulled the pins out of her hair and began to stroke it rhythmically, his hands passing over its silkiness with infinite gentleness. 'You're such a little thing,' he muttered. 'And so very sweet. I need you badly, you know, Sue.'

She tried to hang on to sanity. 'I guess you do,' she said with a travesty of a laugh, pretending to misunderstand. 'If all your Mrs Bensons walk out on you at the drop of a hat.'

'I need you,' he said again. 'I want you. I think I've wanted you from the first moment I saw you in Tokyo. You knocked me off balance.'

You're telling me *you* were knocked off balance, Sue wanted to laugh hollowly. *I* was the one who was knocked off balance and I've been staggering ever since. But somehow she had to play this light. A man and a girl alone together—shaded lights, logs crackling. Of course he would make a pass at her, why not? In his world it would be the accepted thing to do. It wouldn't mean a thing to him. But to her it would mean more than physical surrender. It would mean total surrender of the whole of herself for the rest of her life. That was a commitment she shrank away from.

'You had a funny way of showing it,' she said,

laughing unevenly. 'First you accused me of being a tart, and then you acted rather like a jailer carting me off to prison. And when I lay on the edge of your bed rather than turn you out when you seemed ill you gave me some very dirty looks afterwards.'

He laughed, lying back in his chair. 'Was I really as bad as all that?'

'You certainly were. At the beginning anyway. You improved slightly later on.'

'I told you you knocked me off my balance,' he said, 'That accounts for all my erratic behaviour.'

Does it, Sue thought hazily? I wonder if it does.

She tried to think of something else to say but nothing came. Luke was silent too. The only sound was of the logs crackling and settling down in the grate. Panic began to rise in Sue. She clutched the handle of her coffee cup with tense fingers.

'Sue——'

An odd note in his voice made her look up and she found she couldn't look away again. In the dim light their eyes held each other and she felt a sudden strong stirring inside. Her hands began to shake and her coffee slopped over into the saucer.

'Put that down,' Luke said, very deep, and she put the coffee cup down on the floor, moving jerkily, like a zombie.

'Now come over here.'

'Wh-where?' she whispered. There wasn't more than a couple of feet between their two chairs.

'Here.' He took both her hands and pulled her on to his knees and she couldn't have resisted if her life had depended on it. She felt as if she were dissolving into the hardness and warmth of his body. The tension left her as she breathed out a long sigh and she curled up in his arms like a kitten. This, she thought dimly, was all part of coming home.

That was the last coherent thought she had for some time. There was a blaze inside her to match the blazing logs on the fire and she was melting like wax in Luke's arms. She turned her mouth up to his and as their lips met and clung she passed into another world that was all tingling, throbbing feeling. She felt him start to tremble against her as his hand found its way beneath her woollen jumper and expertly unfastened the catch of her bra, to close over her breast, caressing with featherlike strokes the nipple that hardened under his touch.

This was a totally new experience for Sue, new and intoxicating. She hardly realised how far she was responding; it was completely natural that she should fumble to unbutton his shirt with feverish hands, that she should tangle her fingers in the mat of hair beneath, while all the time her mouth was moving on his almost frantically.

It was like a physical pain when he suddenly pushed her away from him so that she ended up in a heap on the sheepskin rug in front of the fire. He kept one arm around her, supporting her or she would have fallen. With the other hand he leaned down and picked up his glass.

He took a swig and put it down again. Then he said, his voice steady, 'Let sanity prevail for a moment. We have a slight problem. There is only one bedroom prepared—mine. I don't expect you to sleep in a cold room that hasn't been used for months. I could offer you my room and I could make do down here.' He glanced around the small study; there wasn't even a sofa in it.

'Or . . .' he added deliberately. 'There is another possibility which appeals to me more. We could share my bed. It's quite a large one.'

There was a smile in his voice as he added, 'But I

must warn you that this time you may not be allowed to sleep on the edge of the bed. What about it, little Sue?'

He was giving her an opportunity to refuse. In the name of sanity she ought to refuse. But inside Sue, love and lust were blending into a sweet, potent torment. 'Yes,' she whispered. 'Oh yes, yes.'

The bedroom was long and low. The curtains were closed and an electric fire threw a glow over the room. The covers on the big bed were drawn back. Luke must have been up here while she was cooking the supper, Sue thought vaguely. Was he planning this even then? It didn't seem to matter.

He undressed her as she stood in front of the fire. 'Lovely,' he murmured as her white skin pinkened in the glow. 'You're lovely.' Quickly he stripped off his own clothes and took her in his arms and they stood pressed together urgently for a long moment. His hand moved down lower and then, with a little groan, he lifted her and laid her on the bed.

'Warm enough?' he whispered, slipping in beside her.

Warm? She was slowly burning up.

'Am I right—this is the first time for you?' As Sue nodded speechlessly his hands grew more gentle on her. 'Trust me,' he said. 'I'll make it good for you.'

With infinite skill he stroked and caressed her silky flesh, rousing sensations that sent great waves washing over her until she gasped and cried out for a complete union of their two bodies. Her body seemed to move of its own volition beneath his. Her hands clasped him, drawing him down on her as if she couldn't get near enough to him, but although he was in the grip of passion he still could keep enough control of himself to be sure that the pain she felt was so slight as to be almost pleasure, and afterwards that they shared the heights of ecstasy together, to lie back finally, their hearts thumping in unison, exhausted, fulfilled. There were tears in Sue's eyes because it had been so beautiful.

She turned towards him, touching his cheek gently. In the glow of the fire she studied every bit of his face, letting her fingers roam over the high cheekbones, tracing the hollows beneath, the strong jawline, the firm lips that had given her so much pleasure, learning him by heart. 'Oh, that was—was—I never dreamed it could be like that,' she said softly.

He raised himself on one elbow, looking down into her face. 'It can be even better, I promise you.' His voice was tender. He hadn't spoken to her in that tone before but somehow she recognised it. Perhaps she had heard it in her dreams. 'But now you need your sleep—it's been a long day for you—a long and eventful week. Go to sleep, sweet Sue. Good night.'

He kissed her softly and eased her round so that they lay cradled together, his arm loosely around her. 'Good night, Luke—darling,' Sue murmured sleepily. It was the first time she had spoken his name and it felt so good on her lips that she had to say it again. 'Luke—Luke——' She wanted to say 'I love you'. But she didn't know whether she had spoken the words because she was dropping over the edge of sleep.

CHAPTER SIX

SUE woke up with a lazy, delicious feeling that something wonderful had happened. Then memory came and she threw out an arm but she was alone in the big bed. She went cold with panic. Luke had gone, he'd lost interest in her, perhaps last night had disappointed him. He must have had so many women—experienced, sophisticated. How could she have hoped to compete—she, an ingenuous young virgin who had never learnt any of the arts of love? She had to find him; when she saw him she would know the worst—if it *was* the worst.

The big travelling bag that had accompanied her from Australia to Japan and now back to England was sitting beside the wardrobe. Nervously she slipped out of bed and saw the reflection of her pale nakedness in the long mirror, her white-gold hair tousled, her eyes still heavy with love and sleep, and she looked away again quickly, rummaged in her bag and pulled a light wrap round her, fastening the sash tightly.

The room was warm this morning. Pale November sunshine was creeping round the edges of the green brocade curtains. She pulled them back and caught her breath at the view that greeted her. For as far as she could see in both directions Windermere Lake lay spread out below her, a flat expanse of grey water. Mist hovered low over the trees and hills, and all the shrubs in the garden drooped their leaves disconsolately. A fine covering of snow powdered the lawn. It would have seemed a sombre scene, perhaps, to anyone not born and bred in these parts but to Sue it was beautiful beyond belief and the emotion of homecoming brought a great lump in her throat.

If only Luke loved her, what heaven it would be to live here with him. But he didn't love her, he had been quite straight with her about that. Even when he suggested that they should marry he had said, 'You won't expect promises of undying love,' and his tone had been so cynical that she had winced to hear it.

And now? Now she supposed she was his mistress. The idea was quite extraordinary to her. She had often pictured herself a wife, happy and contented, keeping house for a husband, with a garden and a couple of children playing and a baby in a pram. What she hadn't realised until last night was that her sexual needs were so devastating, so utterly irresistible. She knew that Luke would only have to say a word in that deep, husky voice, or put a hand on her, to have her falling eagerly back into his bed.

As eagerly as she had last night. She hadn't put up much of a fight for her maidenly virtue, had she? She felt the heat rising inside as she remembered the uninhibited way she had given herself to Luke. Auntie Meggie would have been shocked and scandalised. But then, Aunt Meggie would have been very surprised if she had read any of the novels that Sue kept in her bedroom. Fortunately, perhaps, Auntie Meggie never had time to read anything. It was from her books alone that Sue had learned about life in the modern world outside the closed little community of Langeroo, where she had been lovingly chaperoned in a way that was almost Victorian.

Sue sighed. Perhaps she should be feeling guilty, but she wasn't. She loved Luke and she had given him willingly what he asked and that was all there was to it.

And now? She had promised Luke to stay and stay she would, whatever the future brought. And now she must get dressed and go downstairs to see what was happening in this household for which, strange though it might seem, she was responsible.

She took a shower in the bathroom that led off the bedroom. Then she opened the wall-cupboard to look for some shampoo. There were bottles of body-lotion, perfumes, powders, a tiny lady-styled razor. She closed the door quickly and washed her hair with clear water under the shower. She wouldn't want Luke to be reminded by the scent of her hair of some other woman he had shared his bed with. She winced a little at the thought but tried to be practical about it. She just wished she weren't such a novice in the love-game; she was horribly afraid she wouldn't be able to hold him. She supposed that a mistress always had that fear.

Back in the bedroom she pulled on denim jeans and a sweater—the only clothes she had which were remotely suitable to wear here—and began to towel her hair dry, but her nerves took over at the thought of seeing Luke again, until her hands were shaking so much that she could hardly hold the towel and she had an empty, sick feeling inside.

When the door suddenly opened she jumped and let out a yelp. Luke appeared in the doorway. 'Good morning, sweet Sue.' He strode over to her, as she sat on the dressing-table stool, and dropped a kiss on her still-damp hair. 'You're trembling, Sue, what's the matter?'

'You—you frightened me, appearing so suddenly,' she stammered.

He grinned. 'Next time I'll shout,' he said. He seemed in high good humour this morning. 'I've been getting the boiler going, the house is warming up now. The oil situation is OK, it was just that idiot Benson woman—she'd switched off the whole system.'

He straddled a small chair, forearms folded along the back of it, watching Sue as she combed out her hair. 'Leave it loose,' he said. 'I like it better that way.'

She twisted the heavy fall of hair into a knot, her fingers fumbling. 'I feel more like a housekeeper if I put my hair up,' she said.

'Do you want to feel like a ... housekeeper?' Luke said, weighting the words heavily.

'Well I—I—that's what I am, isn't it?' The damp knot of hair slipped out of the pins and cascaded into her neck ... She was more conscious every moment of his eyes on her.

The silence that followed her remark stretched into an aching infinity. She struggled to pin up her hair again but at last gave it up and sat staring helplessly into the mirror, trying not to meet his eyes in the reflection there.

But at last she could avoid them no longer and she saw the little smile that creased them at the corners. He said calmly. 'I enjoyed last night. I hope you did too.'

The heat rushed into her cheeks. 'Yes, I—I ...' What a way to put it, as if they were talking about a dinner-date, or a visit to the theatre.

He laughed softly. 'You're a born romantic, little Sue. I'm a realist about such things.' But he hadn't always been a realist. That night in Tokyo when she had slept on the edge of his bed, he had turned towards her in his sleep and his voice had been deep and throbbing with tenderness. 'Van—my love—my darling wife——' Oh yes, he'd been in love once, and that love had left only bitterness. The vulnerable side of him was sealed off. But perhaps—some day—if she made herself indispensable to him——

He swung one long leg over the chair and came and stood behind her. 'We were good together and that's what matters.' His hands came round her from behind and closed over her breasts and she gasped.

He pulled her closer back against him, lifting her hair and nuzzling his mouth into the hollow of her neck. A warm, slow tide of desire began to rise inside Sue.

His mouth was close to her ear. 'I want you again, Sue. Now—*please*.' His voice was urgent. 'We were tired last night. This morning I could make it so much better for you.' He lifted her from the stool and turned her into his arms. 'We're quite alone,' he murmured as he pulled the woollen jumper over her head. 'Chris has gone out for a riding lesson.'

Christopher! Heavens, she'd forgotten all about Christopher. She must be mad. Yes, she *was* mad, mad with a sweet tumult of rising passion. Luke pulled down the zip of her jeans and she stepped out of them, letting them fall in a heap to the floor. I'm wanton, she thought. I'm utterly without shame, and she laughed with the glory of it, unfastening her bra and shivering as Luke's mouth accepted the invitation of the nipples that hardened at the touch of his lips.

With shaking fingers she unfastened the buttons of his shirt and her arms closed round him, drawing him closer so that the roughness of his body hair brushed her soft skin with a delicious sensation that made her move against him instinctively until he groaned aloud and pushed her backwards on to the bed, his mouth moving all over her, devouring her like a starving man.

Suddenly he was still. 'Wait—wait . . .' he muttered. 'I'm rushing you, darling.'

'No,' she cried the word. 'No—please—I don't want to wait.' She was almost sobbing. She felt his hands move down, pulling away the flimsy bit of lace that was her only remaining covering; then his own jeans were dragged away and the exquisite pleasure of last night began again, only better, deeper, more intense. Her face was pressed into his neck as the tide rose for both of them until they cried out as it broke with shattering force, leaving them both drained, their hearts thundering, their bodies entwined, moist and silky.

After a long while he rolled over and lay on his back, pulling the silk counterpane loosely over both of them. He stretched his arms above his head. 'God, I needed that.' His voice held deep satisfaction. 'You're like a draught of cool, clear water, Sue, with your youth and your innocence and your generosity. What day were you born—Friday?'

'What?'

'I mean, were you born on a Friday?'

'I don't know,' murmured Sue, bewildered. 'Why?'

'I think you must have been. You know the old rhyme: Friday's child is loving and giving.'

'Oh that.' She lay back lazily. 'Yes, I remember. I always wanted to be a Monday's child. Monday's child is fair of face. I thought Friday's child sounded rather dull.'

Luke rolled over and took her face between his hands. 'You're fair of face too, my child. And there's nothing dull about being loving and giving. Don't ever change, will you?' There was a grave, intense expression on his dark face. He kissed her lips gently and then, propping himself on one elbow, continued to gaze down at her. 'Don't you think, now, that you might change your mind about marrying me, Sue?'

She stared up at him, her eyes wide. This was the very last thing she had expected. 'W-why do you want to marry me now? You've got me here—that was what you wanted, wasn't it?' She held her breath, her eyes searching his face. If only he would say he loved her!

He lay back, his eyes on the ceiling. 'Because I'm a selfish bastard, I suppose. You're the best thing that's ever happened for me, Sue, and I want to make sure of you, so that I won't lose you again. This last year has been a bloody awful time for me. I want a normal life again. I want to look forward to the weekends—to coming back and finding you here with Chris. Oh, I know you're not in love with me, because you told me so in no uncertain terms back in Kyoto. And as you know, love doesn't enter into my scheme of things. My belief is that love—romantic love—is a sickness, and I want no more of it. It upsets your values, plays havoc with your life. Does that shock you?'

'A little,' she said. 'But maybe I can understand.' She had read lots of books about broken marriages. She said in a whisper, 'You don't think this——' she gestured to the crumpled bed '—has anything to do with love?'

But she knew the answer before she saw him shake his head, very wryly. 'Not a lot.'

After a pause she said, 'You knew this would happen, didn't you? You meant it to?'

'I thought it probably would but not quite so soon or so inevitably.'

She was suddenly overwhelmed with despair. 'You think I'm—easy, I suppose.' Her lower lip began to tremble.

He leaned over her, pinning her down by both her hands so that she couldn't push them into her brimming eyes. 'I think,' he said deliberately, 'that you're everything I want. Will you marry me, Sue?'

She swallowed and struggled without success to free her hands. 'Will you?' he insisted fiercely.

Sue looked up at the dark face that was blurred by her tears. 'Yes,' she said. 'Yes, I'll marry you, Luke.'

'That,' he said deliberately and with satisfaction, 'is

exactly what I've been waiting to hear. We'll make something good of it, Sue, see if we don't.' He bent his head and kissed her firmly on the mouth. Then he slid out of bed. 'Now I suggest we come down to earth and get some breakfast.'

The 'phone rang in the study as they were finishing their last cups of coffee at the kitchen table. Luke went to answer it and Sue began to clear the breakfast dishes into the sink. It was a super kitchen, all very modern with its oak fittings and rows of cupboards, its dishwasher and fridge and washing machine concealed behind matching decor. The wide window looked down over the garden to the lake. Luke's wife would have been the one to choose all this. A green wave of jealousy washed over Sue, and she turned the hot tap on full and squeezed washing-up liquid into the bowl. She would make a better job of it, she vowed. She would make a happy, peaceful home here to welcome him when he came back at weekends. That was what he wanted from her, wasn't it? That, and to be a woman in his bed. It sounded like a picture of an old-fashioned wife. Well, that was all right by her. And some day the hard shell he had built round himself would break. She would *make* it break. She swished the suds in the bowl fiercely and little rainbow bubbles drifted up into the air and burst above her head.

Luke came back into the kitchen, frowning. 'Hell and damnation,' he said.

Sue turned from the sink. 'Something's wrong?'

'Too true,' he groaned. 'That was our esteemed Chairman—it seems there's a special meeting of all the group's directors this evening and probably going on into tomorrow. A big deal has come up that concerns us all. And that means me, I'm afraid. He wants me there particularly—said he rang on the offchance that I was home from Japan.' He ran a hand through his hair. 'I'll have to go, blast it. Oh Lord, what a foul nuisance.'

Sue dried her hands and came over to him. 'A meeting in London? Will you have to drive all the way back?'

''Fraid so.' He glanced at his watch. 'It would have been nice to relax on the train but I doubt if I'd have time to catch the morning express now. And anyway I'd have to get to Lancaster to pick it up.'

'Couldn't I drive you?' Sue offered. This would be part of the role she was visualising for herself: the wife who drives her husband to the station in the morning.

He shook his head absently, his thoughts obviously on the business meeting ahead. 'Drive the Mercedes? I'd have to vet your driving first.' He brought his full attention back to her. 'We'll get the Metro serviced for you so that you can potter around here. But before you can drive anything at all you'll have to get a UK driving licence as you're living in this country permanently.'

He sighed, wrinkling his brows in irritation. 'There's such a hell of a lot to organise.' The way he was looking at her made her feel as if she was an encumbrance that had been wished on him. They might have been back to square one, when they first met in Japan. Sue bit her lip and said nothing.

'Look,' he said at last. 'You go and dig out any papers you've got—passport, birth certificate, Australian driving licence, anything else at all—and I'll let my PA cope with them, she's very efficient.'

Sue had a horrid picture of an elegant young woman with a slinky figure and an effortless grasp of everything important that concerned Luke. 'OK,' she said as cheerfully as she could manage and went up to do as she was asked.

The bedroom was a mess. Hastily Sue pulled the

covers over the bed they had shared last night and again this morning. Luke wouldn't want to be reminded of that now, he had more important things on his mind, she told herself, trying not to feel sick with disappointment at the way things were turning out.

She heard him talking on the 'phone downstairs and by the time he came into the bedroom she had found the papers he wanted, all neatly together in the wallet that she had kept with her ever since she left England four years ago.

'Here they are.' She handed the wallet to him and he glanced through the contents and pushed the wallet into his brief case. 'Right. We can go ahead with plans. We'll be married in London, it'll be more convenient. It should be possible to arrange it for the week after next. I'll come up next weekend and we can drive down to London together on the Monday, after Chris has gone back to school.'

'But—but shouldn't he be there? I thought . . .' Sue began. She was going to be Christopher's stepmother, surely he should be at the wedding.

Luke shook his head. 'Better not. Better to present him with a *fait accompli*. He's got end-of-term exams coming up, I don't want him to be upset.'

Sue smiled faintly. 'Do you think he'll see me as the wicked stepmother then?'

Luke dragged his sweater over his head and began to pull open drawers in a tallboy beside the window. 'That bloody woman—where's she put my clean shirts?' he roared.

There was a nest of small drawers inside the fitted wardrobe, whose sliding door was half open. Feeling very like a wife already, Sue went over and discovered a pile of white shirts in the top drawer. She picked one out and presented it to Luke in silence.

He took it from her. Then, suddenly, he looked at her and actually saw her. 'You really are rather a star, Sue,' he said. 'I'm lucky I've got you.'

Sue felt as if he'd pinned a medal on to her. He put his hands on her shoulders looking down into her face intently. 'I *have* got you, haven't I? I didn't dream it.'

Sue laughed to hide the way her eyes must be giving her away, telling him how much she loved him, how much she wanted to throw her arms round his naked chest and bury her face in the hollow of his neck, where it had rested only an hour ago. 'It seems like it,' she said briskly.

He buttoned his shirt, frowning with exasperation. 'This is a damn nuisance. I wanted to have this weekend with you to get things arranged. I don't like leaving you here on your own when you've only just arrived.'

'I shan't be on my own, there's Christopher,' she reminded him and smiled calmly. 'I'm sure his father's son is capable of defending a lady. And by the way, do I collect Christopher from his riding lesson?'

'If you would.' He jotted an address on a note-pad on the bedside table. 'It's a farm—belongs to Peter Burrows, a friend of mine. Only about a mile down the lane, you can't miss it. You could cut across the field.'

Sue was standing beside the window and he came behind her and pointed the direction, his hand resting loosely on her shoulder. 'There.'

'I'll find it,' she said, moving away quickly.

He sat down on the bed and unzipped his jeans and began to pull them off. Sue felt a burning heat invade her whole body. 'I'll—I'll go and see to things downstairs,' she muttered and fled.

By the time Luke came down, elegant in a dark grey suit, white shirt and striped tie, Sue had herself under control again.

He led the way into the study and tapped a slim red book on the telephone table. 'You'll find the 'phone numbers you might want in here—my flat in Town, and the office number. Oh, and the number of the local garage. You'll have to get Fred to ferry you into Windermere to shop, or wherever else you want to go, until your driving licence comes through. He's an obliging fellow—he'll come to take Chris back to school on Monday morning and you can arrange things with him then. Ask him to get the Metro serviced ready for use too.'

He took out his cheque book, filled in a cheque and handed it to her. 'You can go in and open an account for yourself at my bank in Windermere. And you'll want some ready cash to get anything you need.' He tossed a roll of notes on the desk. I think that's about all. If you get stuck with anything give me a ring at the flat.'

They went out to the car together and he threw his brief-case and camel car-coat on the back seat, and turned to her, frowning. 'I hate to leave you holding the can like this.'

She smiled cheerfully at him. 'In at the deep end! I expect I can cope.'

'Good girl.' He climbed in behind the wheel and started the engine. 'I'll ring you tonight. I don't suppose I'll get back until next weekend, but we'll keep in touch.' He slammed the door and reached for his seat belt.

As he pushed the car into gear Sue stood hugging her arms round her, despair creeping into her bones along with the cold. Was he going to leave her like this? But Luke pushed the gear lever into neutral again and rolled down the window.

'Forgotten s-something?' Sue's teeth were chattering.

'Um.' He stretched out and took her hand and pulled her towards the car. 'This.' He kissed her and his lips were hard and cold. 'That will have to last until I get back.' Then he gave her a little push. 'Go in now—you'll get frozen. Goodbye, Sweet Sue. Think about me.'

Sue watched the car disappear round the bend of the short drive and thought, he's taking part of me with him. I won't be whole again until he comes back. But Luke would be whole enough. Luke Masters was his own man, he wouldn't again let a woman own any part of him. They might share things, be friends, sleep together with heady pleasure, but his heart would remain his own.

It was a bleak thought, but at least she was back in Lakeland, where she wanted to be, and it would have been stupid in the extreme to spend all her days moping. She had the rest of the weekend to get to know Christopher. That was the first and most important thing to tackle, and her heart sank a little at the prospect. It hadn't been a very auspicious first meeting last night, when he had mistaken her for his mother. Obviously he still adored his mother and hoped she would come back. He wouldn't take kindly to having someone here in his mother's place. The wind, blowing across the lake, rustled the dead leaves round her ankles. Sue shivered and pulled her woolly sweater closer round her as she went back into the cottage.

It was a beautiful cottage. Never mind if Luke's wife had chosen everything, Sue had to admit that it was beautiful. The long, beamed living room looked as if it had come straight out of *Ideal Home* magazine: uncluttered, with deep chairs and sofas and sturdy oak furniture, the carpets a muted Berber. The curtains framing a superb view of the lake were an eye-catching splash of colour—a country-garden design of poppies and delphiniums.

She wandered under an archway to the dining part of the room. A table stood in front of the end window and here the view was of the fells, rising and dipping into the distance where the mountains blended mistily into the sky. Sue drew in a deep breath, seeing a summer scene out there instead of the bleakness of the winter. They would linger over dinner here, with the garden scents drifting in through the open window. She would have candles on the table, tall twisty red candles in polished brass holders, and there would be masses of flowers around and Luke would smile at her under those heavy lids and . . .

But it was November and there were no flowers and she could almost hear Luke's voice again, saying, 'You're a born romantic, Sue.' Perhaps she was, and if so she'd better forget it because it wasn't going to get her anywhere with Luke Masters.

Upstairs, she tidied the bedroom she had shared with Luke last night, doing her best to be brisk and businesslike about the job, but unable to stop herself laying her head on the pillow where his dark head had lain. When she managed to pull herself together she transferred everything of her own to a smaller room along the passage which looked like a guest room. This would be her room, at any rate until they were married. After that . . . She felt the heat rising through her body again; she really must begin to get a hold on herself.

She busied herself finding blankets in the airing cupboard and making up the bed. She switched on the electric blanket and unpacked her meagre belongings. It was much too cold here to wear any of the dresses she had taken to Japan. She would have to go into Windermere and buy some thick woolly sweaters and pants and boots; she meant to get out and have a trek over the well-remembered fells at the earliest possible moment.

Christopher's room, when she opened the door and peeped in, was much as she would have expected a nine-year-old boy's room to be: cluttered with books, models, posters, a record-player, a transistor-radio-cum-tape-recorder. There were clothes on chairs and on the floor—football boots—a red dressing gown. Posters of pop stars covered the walls but pinned on a peg-board there was something that drew Sue further into the room: a whole series of drawings of a horse. They were childish and crude but there was something about them that told Sue that they were done with feeling. Christopher loved that horse. She must remember that.

She put the bedclothes straight, careful to move nothing else in the room. She would walk across the fields now and tackle what might be quite a difficult hurdle of her new life—gaining the confidence of Luke's son. She pulled on her short jacket, wishing she had something warmer to wear, and set out.

The overnight snow was melting and the fields were soaking wet. By the time Sue reached the farm in the valley that Luke had pointed out to her her shoes were sodden and her feet were even colder than the rest of her. There was nobody in sight as she picked her way across the muddy yard; a large brown collie dog watched her from a distance as she knocked on the door. There was no answer and after waiting and knocking again she made her way round the side of the house to the sprawling outbuildings. Farmhouses were often deserted at this time of the morning; there was always work to be done outside.

A clucking of hens from one of the sheds sounded hopeful. She pushed open the door and saw a young woman at the far end of the shed, doling out feed into the troughs. 'Hullo,' Sue called. 'May I come in? I've come to take Christopher home.'

The young woman turned. 'Half a mo'' She emptied the last of the feed, slung the bucket over her arm and pushed back a mop of reddish, curly hair as she came towards Sue.

'They're not back yet, I shouldn't think they'll be long. You're new, aren't you? Chris said ...' She broke off, round eyes goggling at Sue. 'It isn't—it can't be ... you're Susan Larkin.'

Sue stared back, her mouth widening into a smile of recognition. 'And you're Mary Forbes.'

'Mary Burrows since last April.' A hand with a wide gold wedding ring was waved in front of Sue's eyes. 'Well, this *is* a nice surprise. Up the old school! Come inside and have some coffee and tell me how the world's been treating you. I thought I'd heard you went to Australia.'

They walked back into the house together. Sue had never known Mary Forbes particularly well—Mary was a year older than Sue and a form higher and she was staying on to take A-levels when Sue left school to go to the Art College—but Sue remembered her as a breezy, outgoing girl, good at games and popular with the staff and the other pupils. It would be lovely to have her for a neighbour.

They settled down in front of the Aga in the big farm kitchen with mugs of coffee and Mary insisted on Sue taking off her shoes and putting them to dry. 'But I don't quite understand,' Mary said, puzzled. 'Christopher was going on about his Daddy bringing back a new housekeeper. I didn't think Mrs Benson would last long. Poor old Luke's had a terrible time getting anyone to stay. It's a bit off the beaten track out here. But how come you've taken to housekeeping,

Sue? I thought you left school to do art—I remember you won the school art prize the year you left.'

Sue filled in a few details of her life for the last four years, and Mary was warmly sympathetic and interested. 'And you met Luke in Australia?'

'Oh no, we met in Japan at my brother's wedding and when Luke discovered that I was longing to come back to Lakeland he offered to bring me back with him to find my roots. And of course I jumped at the chance.'

'Of course.' Mary looked at her rather oddly. And then, 'You know about Luke and the divorce and everything?'

'I know there was a divorce. Luke doesn't talk about it.'

'Well no, he wouldn't, I guess he's trying to put it behind him, but even after all this time he's still pretty shattered. They split up once before but she came back and of course he took her back—he was absolutely crazy about her. But in the end she wanted a divorce and he pretty well went to pieces afterwards. I think we were able to help him through that time a little. He and Peter—my husband—have been friends since they were kids and Luke used to come here whenever he felt like it. Peter and I thought he was well rid of Vanessa but other peoples' opinions don't count at a time like that, do they?' Mary pulled a face. 'I'm talking too much, it's a bad habit of mine, but Luke is apt to get moody at times and it might help you to settle down at Thrang Cottage if you have a general idea of the situation. Is this housekeeper thing meant to be permanent?'

Sue laughed rather awkwardly. 'I hope so. I—you see—Luke and I are going to be married.'

'No!' Mary's amazement was complete. Her mouth fell open, and she collapsed back into her chair. 'Oh

Lord, now I *have* put my foot in it. Why didn't you stop me?'

Then she sat forward and touched Sue's arm. 'But it's marvellous news and I do wish you the very best, my dear. It's just that—that I can't get over it. It's so unexpected. We never thought that Luke would . . .' She shook her head helplessly. 'You must forgive me.'

'Please don't worry. You haven't told me much I don't know already.' But it had hurt to hear it put into words. The way Mary had spoken it sounded as if Luke were *still* crazy about Vanessa.

'Well, anyway, it'll be lovely having you for a near neighbour. I'm thrilled.' Mary spoke warmly. She was probably trying to cover her embarrassment as quickly as she could, but Sue felt sure she meant what she said.

'Me too.' The two girls smiled at each other and Mary said, 'Where is Luke, by the way?'

Sue pulled a face. 'He had to drive back to London this morning. We only arrived last night and the housekeeper had decamped and Christopher was on his own.'

'Oh, you poor dears, you should have come to us. I'd have had the fire lit for you if I'd known. And Chris knows he can come here whenever he likes.' She glanced up at the kitchen clock. 'They should be back from their ride any time now. He's out with Tony, my brother. Tony's staying with us while he's on leave from his engineering job in Kuwait. He goes back next week and then I'm afraid Chris's riding lessons are over for a bit. The riding school is mine, you see, but I'm having to give it up for the winter. A little Burrows due in April,' she explained with a grin.

'Oh, how lovely!' Sue was grateful for the change of subject and they talked babies happily until a clatter of hooves in the yard outside signalled the riders' return.

She said hastily, under her breath, 'Mary, Christopher doesn't know yet—about Luke and me being married, I mean. We only decided this morning and Luke doesn't want Christopher's end-of-term exams to be upset by the thought of a new stepmother.'

'Oh!' Mary looked a little blank. 'Oh, I see. OK then, I'll keep your guilty secret.'

Christopher came rushing into the kitchen, twirling his riding hat, his cheeks rosy, his grey eyes shining under long thick lashes. He looked so like his father that Sue's heart gave a little lurch. 'Oh, that was super,' he began and then stopped as he saw Sue.

'Hullo, Christopher, your father asked me to come over and walk home with you and tell you that he's had to go to London.' She kept her voice pleasantly friendly.

'Oh!' The childish mouth drooped and he turned to Mary. 'Well, if Dad's not at home I needn't go back, need I? Can I stay here, Aunt Mary? And p'raps go for another ride this afternoon?'

'Sorry, Buster, no can do.' A tall young man with curly fair hair strolled into the kitchen and Mary said, 'Sue, this is my incorrigible brother. Tony, meet Susan Larkin, an old school friend of mine. She's staying at Thrang Cottage.'

Tony held Sue's hand longer than was necessary. 'Hullo, Susan.' His eyes creased up appreciatively. 'What a pity!'

'What's a pity?' Mary asked. 'Do you want some coffee?'

'Yes, please.' Tony sank into a chair. 'A pity that I'm going back next week,' he grinned, his eyes on Sue's gold hair and long legs in their tight jeans.

'Tony, behave yourself.' Mary handed him a mug of coffee. 'What would you like to drink, Chris?'

'I don't want anything,' the boy said rather sulkily

and Mary's eyes met Sue's and she shrugged significantly. 'I'll go and rub Flossie down.'

'No need,' Tony told him. 'Joe's seeing to both the horses. The old boy loves 'em, doesn't he?' he said to Mary. 'He'll be lost when they go.'

'Go?' Christopher was suddenly galvanised into suspicion. 'Where are they going, then?'

Tony pulled a face. 'Oh Lord, didn't anyone tell you, chum? Peter's arranged for them to be stabled in Keswick for the winter. There won't be anyone to exercise them here.'

'Keswick? But that's miles away,' wailed Christopher. 'Won't I be able to ride Flossie, then?'

Tony looked at Mary across the boy's head. 'Oh, I expect something will be arranged next spring.'

'But why can't Aunt Mary go on looking after them, she always has?' Christopher's jaw stuck out as he turned to Mary. 'Haven't you?'

'Your aunt's got other things to think about just now.' Tony got up and gave Christopher a push towards the door. 'Come on, chum, home you go. I'll walk across the field with you while my dinner's getting cooked. May I?' he asked Sue, blue eyes dancing mischievously.

'Yes, of course.' She didn't relish the thought of being alone with a disgruntled Christopher at the moment.

She retrieved her shoes from beside the Aga and put them on. 'Come again soon, won't you?' Mary urged as they walked to the door. 'It'll be lovely having you so near, we'll have splendid gossips and I'll tell you all the news about our old mates from school.'

Tony chatted away about his job in Kuwait as they walked across the field and when they reached the cottage he lingered at the gate. Sue thought he would have accepted an invitation to come in but she smiled pleasantly and thanked him for his company, and he set off back the way they had come.

'Come on, let's find something to eat, Christopher.' She went into the kitchen, the boy trailing behind her, flicking at his boots with his riding whip. 'It'll have to be fast-food out of the freezer until I can get into Windermere on Monday to shop.'

Christopher was watching her silently as she pulled off her gaberdine jacket and hung it behind the door.

Suddenly he said, 'Are you really going to stay? They don't usually.'

Sue filled the kettle at the sink. 'No, I've heard you've had trouble with housekeepers.'

'I don't mean housekeepers.'

She spun round. 'What *do* you mean then, Christopher?'

'You know what I mean,' he said, meeting her eyes with a curious, unchildlike stare. 'I know you were in my Dad's bedroom last night. I heard you talking.'

Sue's breath stuck in her throat for a moment. Then, 'I see,' she said slowly. Christopher was nearly ten years old and evidently well-informed about the ways of the world.

'Well then, you may as well know that your father and I are going to be married.' Sorry Luke, but I had to tell him. I'm not going to be labelled as one of the women who visit you here but 'don't stay long'. She saw again, vividly, the bathroom cupboard with its luxurious feminine toiletries.

Christopher had gone very pale. 'I don't believe it,' he said. 'Dad won't marry you, you know.' He was staring at her and he looked so like Luke when he had stared at her at the airport in Tokyo and said, 'Get lost, will you', that she felt suddenly sick.

'Why should I think that?' she said.

Chris shrugged in a very unchildlike way. 'Some of the others did,' he said.

The others? Were those the ones who left the skin lotions in the bathroom cupboard? Sue bit her lip. How did she deal with this? 'Well, he says he will,' she said practically, 'but there are lots of things to arrange so it won't be just yet.'

He glared at her, his lower lip jutting. 'It won't be *ever*.'

'No? Well, we'll have to wait and see, won't we? In the meantime we'd better think about having something to eat. I'll go and raid the freezer.'

She spent a long time in the kitchen, giving Christopher a chance to digest her news, and giving herself time to adjust. She couldn't admit that she was scared because of the way he had taken it, but she was. His reaction hadn't been that of a child, it had had the hostility of an adult. Winning him round wasn't going to be easy. And she wished she could find out exactly what he meant about 'the others' but of course she couldn't ask him.

She found a packet of fish fingers and stuck them under the grill and measured out *Smash* into a basin and peas into a pan. She set the table and opened a tin of apricots. There was a tub of ice cream in the freezer.

When everything was ready she went to look for Christopher. He wasn't in the drawing room, or in the hall. She went upstairs but his bedroom was empty. She walked slowly down the stairs. He couldn't have done anything stupid and dramatic, like running away up into the fells, could he? Sudden fear made her scalp prickle.

When she was at the turn of the stairs she heard the front door open. Christopher's voice said, '—and she got here with Dad last night. She says Daddy is going to marry her. He won't, will he, Mummy? Please say he won't.'

A purring voice said soothingly, 'Darling boy, I should think it's very unlikely.'

Luke's wife! *Ex*-wife, Sue reminded herself, pushing back the illogical fear that gripped her stomach when she saw the woman in the hall below. She was silvery blonde and quite ravishingly beautiful. A pale mink coat hung from her shoulders, draped over a black crêpe dress that even to Sue's untutored eyes proclaimed Paris. A gossamer black chiffon bow was tied loosely round an immaculate chignon, and she wore long black suede boots with slim five-inch heels. The faintest whiff of expensive perfume drifted up to Sue as she stood there as still as a statue, her hand gripping the rail.

'Are you *sure* he won't?' Christopher urged.

His mother placed a hand possessively on his shoulder and diamonds glittered on her long white fingers. Then she looked up to where Sue stood transfixed on the stairs, and her slanting green eyes narrowed as she took in the wind-blown hair, the crumpled jeans, the hand-knitted sweater, the grass-stained shoes, and a little smile of contempt slid over her small, perfect mouth.

'Oh yes, my darling,' she said to Christopher. 'I'm quite, quite sure he won't.'

CHAPTER SEVEN

Sue walked stiffly down the stairs. She wasn't supposed to have heard that exchange with Christopher and thought it best to ignore it.

'You're Christopher's mother? I'm Sue Larkin. How do you do?' Managing, with an effort, to keep her voice calm she held out a hand. 'I'm sorry you didn't let us know you were coming. I'm afraid there's only fish fingers for lunch. Luke and I arrived back late yesterday evening and there hasn't been time to shop yet.'

Green eyes slid over Sue and away again as the woman ignored the extended hand. 'Not to worry, we shan't be stopping for lunch.' She gave Christopher a little push. 'You go and change out of those muddy clothes, darling, and we'll drive somewhere and have a civilised meal—just the two of us. Hurry now.'

Christopher dashed up the stairs and Vanessa hitched her fabulous mink coat closer round her shoulders and drifted past Sue into the living room. 'The heating system hasn't been improved, I notice,' she drawled, shivering affectedly. She walked over to a side-cupboard and threw open a door to disclose a selection of bottles and glasses.

'The end of the gin,' she tipped out the last of a bottle and glanced over her shoulder towards Sue. 'You'd better order some more, hadn't you?' She strolled across to the big picture window. 'My God, what a ghastly depressing place this is!' The heavily-mascaraed eyes moved across the grey expanse of lake below and the scarlet mouth curved disdainfully.

'Luke needs his head examining to hang on to a place like this and I shall tell him so when I get back to Town.'

She turned to Sue and stared insolently. 'You're the new housekeeper, I take it? Making hay while the sun shines, is that it? I hear that dear Luke makes quite a habit of bringing what he calls his *housekeepers* up here. Very convenient for his weekends!'

Sue's inside was trembling violently but somehow she kept her voice steady. She took a couple of steps towards the other woman. 'Look, Mrs Masters—or are you Mrs something else by now? I don't know you, I don't like you and I strongly resent the way you're behaving and your tone of voice. Luke has left me in charge here while he's away, and it would be quite within my rights to ask you to leave but as you're Christopher's mother I can't do that. If you take him out you'll be responsible for bringing him back safely. Is that understood?'

Green eyes narrowed and Sue saw a dangerous glint in them, but the purring voice was well under control as the woman shrugged gracefully. 'I really couldn't care less whether you like me or not, my dear. I can't help feeling a little sorry for you, and for the rest of Luke's *housekeepers*. A rich divorced man is such a catch and the poor dears are always so hopeful. As for bringing my son back—I'll do that just when it suits me. Ah—there you are, darling . . .' as Christopher ran into the room, having changed out of his riding boots and brushed his hair. 'Let's be going then, shall we?'

At that moment the 'phone rang in the study. Luke! thought Sue in panic as she hurried to answer it, what on earth am I going to say to him? But the voice on the other end of the line was a light, laughing man's voice, nothing like Luke's deep tones. 'Is that Sue? Tony here. Look, I've had an idea. My date's been cancelled and I thought you might bring young Chris over and he can have another ride, and then perhaps he could stay with Mary, and I could take you out to dinner somewhere. What about it?'

Christopher was standing close behind her. 'Is that Tony? Is it?' He was almost hopping up and down with excitement. 'What does he say? Can I go out on Flossie again?'

'Hold on a minute, please, Tony.' Sue turned to the boy. 'Tony says he can take you out again this afternoon if you like. Do you want to go?'

'Yes, oh yes, please. Mummy, I can go, can't I, and you can come and see me ride. You haven't seen how well I can ride now.' He grabbed the 'phone from Sue. 'Hullo, Tony, super, I can come over this afternoon. Thanks a lot. 'Bye.' He rattled the receiver back on its cradle.

His mother, standing in the doorway, was regarding him with tolerantly raised brows. 'Darling! What *is* all the excitement about?' She smoothed back the boy's dark hair. 'We're going out together for the afternoon, remember? Mummy's come all the way from London to see you, we don't want to bother with anyone else, do we? I'm sure you ride beautifully and you can show me another time.'

'But . . .' Christopher's mouth drooped.

'No buts,' his mother teased. 'Come along. Perhaps we can find some horses somewhere else. I seem to remember there's a riding school near the hotel where we're going for lunch. We can go and look at the horses there. You'd like that wouldn't you? And perhaps you could have a ride.' She put a firm hand round Christopher's shoulders and led him, not very willingly out to a low white car that was standing in the drive.

Sue watched them go with troubled eyes. There was

nothing she could do—nothing at all. She couldn't have stopped Christopher's mother taking him out, could she? She wondered what Luke would think about it and had horrible thoughts about divorced people—sometimes women, sometimes men—who snatched a child away from the parent who had custody because of frustrated love and longing. Somehow that didn't seem to apply in this case. Still, she thought painfully, Luke had left her in charge and she would feel happier if he knew what was going on. She went into the study and dialled the number of his flat in London. An answering machine said, 'This is Luke Masters speaking. Sorry I was out when you rang. If you would please leave your name and telephone number I will . . .'

Even on a machine Luke's voice had the power to stir her inside uncomfortably. After a moment she gathered her wits together and replaced the receiver without leaving a message. She mustn't panic. After all, there was no reason why Christopher's mother shouldn't take him out. She must be very fond of her son to come all the way up here to see him. *Or had she expected to see Luke?* As she turned to the door Sue's eye caught a framed photograph on the top of the big roll-top desk. The light wasn't good in here but even before she leaned nearer she knew it was of Vanessa. It was a sensual, sensational photograph. Delicate wisps of some filmy material concealed very little. Creamy arms were folded over an almost naked breast, allowing a titillating curve to show where the arms crossed. The beautiful lips were moistly parted and great greenish eyes smouldered with a message that promised untold pleasures.

Sue walked away, her legs leaden. No wonder Luke was still 'shattered', as Mary had told her. A woman might consider that photograph vulgar but in the books that Sue had read a man always fell for blatant sexuality. How could she hope to replace a woman like that?

'Love is a sickness,' he had said. But he had kept the photograph on his desk. It looked as if he hadn't got over the sickness, didn't it?

As she stood pondering this new and frightening idea a faint smell of burning came to her. Heavens, the fish fingers! She rushed into the kitchen but it was too late. A thin black haze drifted from the grill pan. Even turned low the grill had done its worst with the fish fingers. Sue tipped the charred remains into the waste-bin and threw open the window, cursing ex-wives who turned up at lunch time and threw their weight about in such a disgusting manner.

What, she wondered, did the beastly Vanessa hope to gain by being so insulting to her? She decided that Luke's ex-wife was a very unpleasant character and that he was well rid of her—even if he did keep her photograph on his desk.

She kept coming back to the thought of the photograph as she made coffee and buttered a couple of rather soggy crispbreads for her own solitary lunch. She carried the tray into the big living room, where she could sit and look out at the fabulous view of the lake. But the happy dreams of the morning refused to come back. She felt lonely and uneasy and found herself fighting a dark, heavy feeling deep inside that probably she had been mad to get herself into this situation. In an effort to divert her thoughts she fiddled with the stereo and managed to get the one o'clock news, which did absolutely nothing to cheer her up. But before it was over the front door bell rang. Surely not Christopher and his mother back already?

But it was Tony Burrows who stood outside the door, his curly fair hair blowing in the breeze, his mouth widening into a grin as he saw Sue. 'Am I too early? I thought I'd drive over and pick you and Chris up and save you the trek over the fields.'

'Oh goodness!' Sue's hand went to her mouth in dismay. 'I'm terribly sorry, but I'm afraid Chris won't be able to ride with you. His mother turned up and she's taken him off with her for the afternoon. Oh dear, how rude of me—I should have rung back and let you know. I *am* sorry.'

The grin on Tony's face didn't diminish by a fraction, if anything it widened. 'Don't be sorry,' he said cheerfully. '*You're* still here. How about taking Chris's place and coming riding with me? You do ride?'

'Oh yes.' On an Australian cattle station everyone rode; it was something Sue had learned very early on in her new life and one thing she had enjoyed greatly about it. 'I'd love to,' she said but added doubtfully, 'but I don't think I should be away from the house. Chris and his mother might come back any time and when they do I must be here. I don't . . .'

I don't trust that woman, was what she had nearly said but that sounded melodramatic and Tony couldn't be expected to know the ins and outs of Luke's marriage failure. She added rather lamely, 'I don't want Christopher to think there's nobody here when he gets home.'

Tony gave her a keen look. 'No, I can well understand that.' Perhaps he knew more than she thought. 'Well, how about if I go back and bring the two horses here and we could have a quick turn over the fells, not far from the house? We could keep an eye on the road—you can see for miles if a car is coming up this way.'

'Well, if you're sure . . .' Sue allowed herself to be persuaded. It would be lovely to ride here, on the fells.

She had always longed to ride here and had envied the riders when she was a small girl. It had been one of Daddy's plans to save up enough money to buy her a pony and riding lessons, but it had never happened.

Tony drove away furiously and was back inside ten minutes, riding a handsome chestnut mare and leading a pretty, paler-coloured filly. 'Mother and daughter,' he explained. 'Rosie and Flossie. Flossie is very sweet-natured.' Blue eyes twinkled at Sue. 'You two have a lot in common, you should get along splendidly together. I've borrowed Mary's hat and a pair of boots for you in case you haven't any here.'

Flossie was a darling; Sue could well understand Christopher's passion for her, and she enjoyed every minute of the ride, not least Tony's admiration of the way she handled the filly. They rode for an hour and not once were they out of sight of the road. Then, at last, Sue caught a glimpse of a white car snaking up the winding ribbon of road. 'Here they are,' she shouted and set off at a gallop towards the cottage. She arrived and dismounted just before the car pulled up outside the front door.

Christopher was out of the car in a flash. 'Flossie,' he yelled and reached up to fondle the filly's nose. 'Oh, Flossie, I've missed you.' He groped in his pocket for a sugar lump from the supply he evidently kept there.

Tony rode up to them. 'Hello, Buster.' He grinned down at Christopher. 'Too late for a ride today. Maybe tomorrow. Want to hack back home with me? Go and get your hat, then.' He glanced at Sue. 'I'll bring him back in half an hour, OK?'

Christopher rushed into the cottage and Vanessa got out of the car and strolled across the drive. 'Hullo, Tony, back from the far ends of the earth?' she drawled. The way her green eyes passed over the young man and the slight sway of her body was frankly provocative. She was evidently a woman who saw every male as a sexual challenge, and Tony looked very handsome in his riding gear, seated up there on the mare. He had pulled off his hat and his fair hair curled attractively round his bronzed cheeks.

But he didn't dismount and Sue thought he looked faintly uncomfortable. 'That's right,' he said. 'How are you, Vanessa?'

Her reply was drowned by Christopher's whoop of 'Tally-ho!' as he came rushing out of the cottage, pulling his riding hat over his dark hair.

'I'll show you how well I can ride, Mummy.' He looked eagerly at his mother. 'Will you give me a leg up?'

Vanessa shuddered. 'Darling! I'm not a stable girl, you know.' She smiled at him, making the words into a joke, but Sue saw the wave of disappointment that crossed the boy's face and she stepped forward and held out her hand.

'Up you go,' she said cheerfully. Christopher hesitated for a moment and then his yearning to get on to the filly won. 'Thanks,' he mumbled and allowed Sue to help him to mount.

'*Chris!*' For the first time there was a petulant edge to Vanessa's voice as she spoke to her son. 'I'm leaving now—aren't you going to say goodbye to me?'

'Oh.' Christopher's face fell. 'I thought you'd stay and watch me ride.'

'Another time.' Vanessa hardly bothered to conceal her boredom now. She had obviously accepted the fact that Christopher's attention was not likely to be diverted from his horse. 'Goodbye, darling, I'll see you again soon.'

'Goodbye, Mummy.' Christopher remembered his manners enough to add, 'And thank you for taking me

out.' In the same breath, 'Come on, Tony, race you.'
And he set off at a brisk canter across the field.

Sue was left with Vanessa, who walked back
towards her car, annoyance showing in every movement of her well-cared-for body. Sue followed at a
distance. I am *not* going to offer her tea, or anything
else, she resolved. Not that Vanessa would have
accepted it, she guessed. She was already swinging
open the door of the smart white car. Before she got in
she turned to Sue.

'I'll say goodbye—I doubt if you will still be here
next time I come to see my son. Housekeepers don't
last long around here.'

It was probably unwise to cross swords with a
woman like this but Sue couldn't resist it. 'Oh, I think
it's quite likely that Luke and I will be married by
then,' she said smoothly, her blue eyes as cold as ice.

'*Really?* They do say hope springs eternal, don't
they? You probably haven't yet discovered Luke's
little ploy. Offering marriage comes quite easily to
him, but he's an adept in wriggling out of it at the last
moment, when he's got what he wants. He charms
some poor deluded woman into looking after his house
in this abysmal spot—*and* gets a bit of nooky on the
side too. You surely don't imagine you've got what it
takes to hold a man like Luke Masters, do you?' The
contemptuous green eyes swept Sue from head to foot.
One hand on the car door, Vanessa added, 'As a
matter of fact I've been thinking recently that I might
even take him back myself.' She smiled a secret smile.
'I can get him back any time I like, you know.'

She slid gracefully into the driving seat, turned the
ignition key and the next moment the white car was
disappearing down the drive with a spurt of gravel.
Sue's legs would hardly take her back to the house and
when she got there she went into the kitchen and stood

beside the table, hanging on to the edge of it, shivering. She didn't believe a word of it, she told herself. Luke wasn't capable of behaving like that.

How do you know? a voice inside her seemed to be saying. How long have you known him? What do you know about him?

Only that he saved Steve's life. Only that I love him.

Nothing has changed, she assured herself, he will telephone tonight and talk about our wedding and everything will be all right again. She must trust Luke, must believe in him, because she had nobody else to turn to. And if you loved someone you trusted them, didn't you?

The 'phone rang in the study and her heart missed a beat but it was Mary. 'Tony and Chris are here,' she said, 'and they're both raring to tuck into a huge tea. Tony's coming over to collect you and we can all tuck in together—right?'

'Oh but—I'm expecting a call from Luke this evening. I don't think I should . . .'

'It's only just after four, you'll be back long before this evening,' Mary insisted. 'Do come.'

The alternative was to sit here alone with her worries. 'I'd love to,' Sue said. 'Thank you.'

It was a happy family at tea in the Burrows's big farm kitchen. Sue met Mary's husband, a big, quiet man who reminded her a little of Ross, and Mary and Tony's good-natured sparring kept the light-hearted atmosphere going. Christopher was bright-eyed and eager whenever the talk turned to horses and Sue guessed that he was trying to find out whether the horses were to be moved for the winter, but if so nobody was telling him for sure.

By the time Sue and Chris got home again Sue thought the boy's hostility towards her might have been softening a little, but he still answered her questions with Yes and No, and volunteered nothing of his own. Once he was alone with her she thought he seemed unhappy, but there was no way she could approach him or offer to help just now. She would just have to wait and hope for the best.

It was nearly midnight when Luke 'phoned and Christopher had been in bed for hours. Sue had lit a fire in the big living room because she didn't want to sit in the study and have Vanessa's photograph staring down at her like a threat. There was an extension 'phone in here so when Christopher had departed upstairs she threw a couple more logs on the fire, pulled up a big easy chair and turned on the TV. She was watching the late movie with about one-tenth of her attention when the 'phone buzzed.

She leapt across the room and snatched off the receiver. 'Hullo?' she said breathlessly.

'Sue, sorry I'm so late, were you asleep?'

Her heart started its wild thudding at the sound of Luke's deep voice. 'Hullo, Luke. No, I was watching TV.' Friendly. Pleasant. No hint that she'd been in an emotional no-man's-land since he left this morning. 'How are things with you?'

'Exhausting. We've been talking all evening and it goes on tomorrow. What's been happening at your end? Have you been coping?'

'Oh, it's been quite an eventful day. I went to pick up Chris, like you said, and had a pleasant surprise. I found that Mary Burrows is an old schoolmate of mine, so we had quite a reunion.'

'Mary? Yes, she's a jolly good sort, you two should get along well.'

'And I met Tony, her brother, the one who's been giving Chris riding lessons.'

'Tony?' he said sharply. 'But I thought Mary

herself was doing that—it's her own venture, the riding school.'

'She's having to pack it in for the winter, she's having a baby, she told me. Tony's staying with them and he's been standing in for her with the riding lessons. He's a delightful young man and Chris gets on very well with him.' She chattered on, wondering, in the back of her mind, how she was going to bring in the fact of Vanessa's visit without making it sound too important. 'Christopher was going riding with Tony again this afternoon, but then your wife—your ex-wife, I mean, turned up and took Chris out to lunch, so of course he couldn't go. So Tony and I had a short ride instead, and . . .'

'Vanessa turned up? Do you mean *Vanessa?*' Luke sounded almost shocked.

'That's right, she turned up before lunch, and——'

'And you let Chris go off with her?'

'Well—yes . . .' Sue faltered. She wished she could see his face.

'Why the blazes wasn't I told what was going on?'

Sue swallowed hard. 'Well, I did wonder if I should try to contact you, but——'

'But you were too busy entertaining this Tony fellow, is that it? Damn it, Sue, you're supposed to be looking after Chris, not letting him go swanning off without you.' He sounded furious.

'But—but she's his *mother*,' wailed Sue. 'What was I supposed to do, for heaven's sake?'

There was a silence and she thought he had rung off. Then he said wearily. 'OK, let's drop it. Anything else to report?'

'No . . . sir.'

'What did you say?' he barked.

'I said "No, sir." Everything is in order.'

There was a shorter silence. Then, 'Don't be stupid, for God's sake, Sue. I wasn't blaming you.'

'Weren't you? I thought it sounded as if you were.'

'OK, take offence if you want to,' he snapped. 'I don't propose to continue this conversation over the 'phone. Ring me back when you're in a more reasonable frame of mind.' There was a sharp click and the brrh at the other end of the line sounded like a rejection.

Sue replaced the receiver, her hand shaking violently. Unreasonable, she thought hotly. *Me*, unreasonable! Mary Burrows had said that Luke was moody. Too true he was moody.

But why had he been so angry because Vanessa had come here? Was it because he wanted to see her himself and had been annoyed that he had missed her? Had he, perhaps, been hoping that she would make some sign that she wanted them to get together again?

And where did she, Sue, fit into the picture?

Tears of confusion and disappointment pricking behind her eyes, Sue switched off the TV and went upstairs to bed. She was beginning to be sorry that she had ever got herself into this situation. Even the joy of being back in her beloved Lakeland wasn't worth the pain of loving a man who didn't and, it seemed, never would love her.

As if Lakeland itself were trying to cheer her up, the weather changed and the following day, Sunday, was glorious. The sun shone out of a brilliant blue sky, where puffy little white clouds chased each other across the tops of the mountains and the waters of the lake rippled with silver and the grazing sheep stood like small carved statues against the deep green of the fells.

Tony appeared early at the cottage. 'Mary's laid on

a riding day for the three of us,' he announced. 'She says we may not get another day like this for months. She's got a packed lunch for us and there's a good mount for you, Sue, and Chris can have Flossie, of course, and we can trek over towards Ambleside and have a picnic and then make our way back. OK?'

Sue had only to look at Chris's ecstatic face to know what her answer must be. Perhaps Mary had guessed that Sue was going to confront difficulties in her new life and was tactfully doing her best to help. But whether it was Mary's doing or not, the atmosphere had improved wonderfully between herself and Chris by the time the riders clattered back into the stable yard, tired and happy, that afternoon.

But Mary's thoughtful hospitality was not over yet. Showers were provided for the three riders, and then a lavish high tea was laid on once again. It was nearly six o'clock, and quite dark, by the time Sue insisted regretfully that she and Chris must go home.

'Chris has to go back to school early tomorrow morning, don't you, Chris? You'll have to tell me what you need to take with you, I'm just a beginner about these things.' She grinned at Chris, willing him to smile back and her heart lifted when he did.

'Thank you for everything, Mary, you're an angel,' Sue whispered, when Tony and Chris had gone out to the car. 'You don't know how much today's helped.'

'My pleasure,' Mary said knowingly. 'Come again soon—and if there's anything I can do . . .'

'Come on, Sue,' yelled Chris, from the car. It was the first time he had called her by her name and it sounded good. Sue hurried out.

'Do I get asked in for a drink?' Tony demanded as the car approached Thrang Cottage. She and Tony were in the front, and Chris was bouncing about tirelessly on the back seat.

'Oh *yes*,' Chris invited his hero enthusiastically. But Sue couldn't reply because her throat had suddenly locked and her heart was thumping like mad.

A long, dark car stood in the drive. All the lights in the cottage were on and the front door was flung open as Tony drew up outside. Luke strode across the gravel and gave Sue a hard look as she slid out of the front seat. 'So you've thought fit to bring Chris home at last, have you?' he said nastily.

'Luke—what a lovely surprise. We didn't expect to see you today, did we Chris?' Sue's greeting sounded patently false but Christopher was too young to notice any 'atmosphere'. He jumped out and hugged his father excitedly. 'Daddy, we've all been riding and Tony says I'm improving by leaps and bounds. P'rhaps I'll be able to leap over some fences soon.' He burst into peals of laughter, delighted with his own joke. Sue prayed silently that Luke wouldn't put him down and he didn't. 'We'll have to see about that,' he said. 'And who is Tony?'

Tony jumped out of the car, extending a hand. 'Tony Forbes, sir. Mary Burrows's brother. I don't think we've met. I've been staying with Mary and Peter this last week and helping young Chris with his riding.'

'Ah!' Luke looked the young man up and down and took his hand briefly, not smiling. 'I'm obliged to you.'

'Tony's coming in for a drink.' Christopher tugged at his father's hand. 'Then he can tell you some more. Auntie Mary says they may have to send the horses away but Tony thinks——'

'That's enough, Chris. Go along in now,' Luke cut in. 'Thank Tony for your lesson.'

'But I thought——'

'Do as I tell you,' rapped out his father.

Chris, hanging his head, murmured, 'Thank you, Tony.'

Tony grinned down at him. 'A pleasure, Buster. Cheero then, Sue. We had a good day, didn't we?'

'Lovely,' murmured Sue. 'Thank you for taking me.'

'Good night, sir, nice to have met you.'

Luke nodded and Tony, not in the least quelled, climbed back into the car and, with a cheery salute, drove off. Sue glanced up at Luke's face as they walked back into the cottage. It was like a thundercloud and for the first time she began to feel a discontent that was not quite resentment at the way he was treating her. She'd done her best since he left. Everything was ticking over; Chris was safe and sound; the cottage hadn't burnt down. So what was the matter with Luke?

Chris was nowhere to be seen. He'd probably gone off upstairs to get out of the way, and the thought came to her that he must know all about his father's moods. Sue made for the kitchen, saying rather stiffly, 'Are you hungry? Shall I cook you something?'

He put a hand on her arm. 'Oh, for God's sake, Sue, don't get on your high horse. Look, I don't want anything to eat.' He urged her into the living room and went over to pour himself a drink. Sue pulled the curtains, straightening them carefully. She had banked down the fire before they left, earlier, and it was still glowing faintly red, so she went down on her knees and poked it gently, persuading some small logs to break into a blaze, drawing out the job to gain time to adjust to Luke's sudden appearance, which had left her feeling weak and trembly.

Luke had sunk into a chair with his drink. 'When you've quite finished being a housekeeper, come and sit down, I want to talk to you.' He sounded as if he were at the end of his tether and although Sue hadn't the faintest idea why, she wasn't going to argue with him in this mood.

'Now,' he said, when she was sitting in a chair opposite. 'I want you to tell me about Vanessa. When she came, how long she stayed, how she looked . . .'

Sue's eyes widened. Shock was like a punch in the stomach. So it was true, what she had feared! He must have been hoping against hope, all these months, that one day Vanessa would come back to him, as she had before. And now she had come and he hadn't been here! No wonder he was in a mood.

Sue sat very still, her nails digging into her palms to stop herself from howling, facing the answer to all her wonderings about Luke. Deep down she thought she'd known this ever since Mary had said, 'Luke was absolutely shattered when she left him'; since Sue had seen the photograph on his desk.

Luke was still in love with Vanessa.

'Well?' he prompted her. 'Come on, Sue, she must have made *some* sort of impression on you.'

That was a laugh, wasn't it? Sue said woodenly, 'Well—she arrived just before lunch and said she was going to take Chris out. She stayed about ten minutes, just to give him time to tidy himself up. She looked . . .' Sue glanced at Luke's face for some sort of reaction, but it told her nothing. 'She looked very beautiful, and very expensively dressed. That's all I can tell you.'

Luke got up and started to pace up and down the room. 'What else? What did she say to you?'

Oh no, Luke, I'm not going to give you the satisfaction of criticising your bitch of an ex-wife. I wouldn't sink to her level.

She shrugged. 'Nothing much. She took it for granted I was the housekeeper.'

He stopped pacing and stood staring down at her, frowning in a puzzled sort of way. Finally he said, 'And what time did she leave when she brought Chris back?'

Sue pretended to search her memory—as if every second of that encounter wasn't already printed on it indelibly. 'Oh, I suppose it was about four. It was beginning to get dark.'

He nodded absently. 'She was probably staying overnight with the Durants, across the valley. Cynthia Durant was a great pal of Vanessa's.' He dropped into the chair again, shrugging. 'Oh well, there's nothing I can do about it at the moment. Can I take you up on your offer of some food, Sue? I can't remember when I last had a meal. There were snacks laid on after the meeting but I skipped that. I wanted to get up here quickly and find out what was going on.'

Yes, of course, you *would*, Sue thought numbly. Perhaps you hoped she would come back again today and you would catch her before she left.

She made for the door. 'Would a couple of fried eggs be acceptable?'

He gave her an absent smile. 'Super, if it's not too much trouble.' He seemed to be making an effort to bring himself back from some private place in his mind. He came across the room after her and put a hand round her shoulder. 'Sweet Sue, I have landed you in a muddle of a situation, haven't I?'

She turned to face him. 'Why?' she said, and he couldn't know how much the little smile cost her. 'I thought I was managing rather well, on the whole. Chris didn't take to me at first, but I think he's coming round now. We both love horses and that means a lot.'

He looked down steadily into her eyes, both hands on her shoulders now. 'You're such an innocent, Sue,' he said. 'Do you truly think you're going to be happy here?'

It was a sick feeling, like going down in a lift. 'Are you thinking of giving me the sack?' she asked with terrible brightness.

'I'm thinking,' he said, not smiling back, 'that I should never have brought you here. Now that Mrs Benson has decamped it'll mean that you'll be alone in the house when Chris is away at school, and I can't allow that.'

'I don't mind a bit,' she said. 'This place isn't strange to me, it feels like home already. Our cottage was only a mile or two away from here. I wouldn't be scared of being alone.'

'*You* may not be scared,' he said. 'But *I* should be. No, it won't do at all.'

Another minute and he'd be saying, very kindly no doubt, that he was going to make other arrangements for her—perhaps send her back to Australia, or to Steve in Japan. She had to think of something quickly. Anything—*anything* to stop him saying that, to gain a reprieve. 'Well, why shouldn't I go over to the farm to sleep? I'm sure Mary would find me a bed somewhere—on a sofa or any-where—then I could come back here in the mornings and get on with things.' She felt as if she were pleading for her life.

'No,' he said sharply. 'That wouldn't be a good idea. I'd prefer to be independent.'

'But Mary's a friend . . .' she argued.

'No,' he said again. 'I'll take a room for you at a small guest house in Windermere—I know the woman who runs it—Mrs Lloyd; she'll make you comfortable. Meanwhile we'll try to get someone to live in. A married couple, perhaps.'

Sue could feel foolish tears welling up behind her

eyes and she turned her head away. 'I'm always being a nuisance to you, aren't I?' she said chokily.

He put a finger under her chin and turned her face towards him. 'Don't ever say that again, Sue.' He looked deep into her eyes, then he put his arms round her and drew her against him, smoothing her hair with infinite gentleness, just as if she had really been a child. 'Poor little Sue,' he said quietly.

She must prove to him that she wasn't a child, that she was a woman—and the woman he had asked to marry him. She wondered if he had forgotten that. She lifted her head and smiled into his eyes. 'All right, I won't,' she murmured and she put her hands round his neck and drew down his head and laid her mouth against his.

She felt a quiver run through his body and pressed against him more closely. 'Luke?' Her lips parted softly in invitation.

His arms moved down, to her waist, to her hips, and he held her against him so hard that she gasped. For a long moment they stayed like that, his mouth enclosing hers, his lips almost brutal in their assault.

Then, with a little groan, he pushed her away. 'No, Sue,' he said. 'Not now. I've got to get back almost immediately.'

'You're going—now? When you've only just come? Oh *no*,' she wailed. His rejection was a physical pain, burning through her. He would have taken her if he had had time, but there were far more important things on his mind.

He walked away and stood with his back to her, running his fingers through his dark hair. 'I must,' he said. 'I shouldn't have come at all, but I had to find out what was going on here. I've got a big meeting on tomorrow morning and there's a stack of work I must do when I get back to London tonight, in preparation for it. If I'm lucky I'll have a couple of hours' sleep afterwards. So you see . . .' He turned to her, spreading out his hands apologetically. 'Forgive me, Sue, and try to understand.'

'I think I do understand,' she said dully. She hoped her legs would carry her to the kitchen. 'I'll get your meal as quickly as I can.'

'That's my girl. I'll ring Mrs Lloyd at the guest house while you're doing that, and then I'll have a quick bite and be off again.' If she had got inside his defences for a moment or two, it was over now, he was completely in control of himself.

All that Sue could think of as she broke eggs into the spluttering fat in the frying pan was that if it had been Vanessa who had asked him to stay, he wouldn't have refused and the certainty of that was cutting her into little pieces.

Luke came into the kitchen and she put the plate in front of him with butter and hunks of brown bread. 'Thanks, Sue, you're a star, as I've said before.' He reached up and touched her pale cheek gently. 'I'm being a selfish brute just now, but I've got a hell of a lot on my mind.'

The kettle boiled and she turned away, biting her lip. It was almost the last straw—that he should feel sorry for her.

Half an hour later Luke had gone, with a brief goodbye to Christopher, up in his room, and an even briefer goodbye to her, and a promise to keep in touch.

He had arranged that Sue should stay at the guest house until some living-in domestic could be found. He had also arranged by 'phone for the garage man, Fred, to ferry her backwards and forwards to the town until her driving licence came through. Luke was very good at organising things, Sue thought miserably as she cleared up the kitchen. She wondered if he had organised the little matter of their wedding yet. If so, he hadn't mentioned it, and she had been unable to bring herself to ask. Vanessa's words kept ringing in her ears. 'Offering marriage comes quite easily to him but he's an adept at wriggling out of it at the last moment.'

He *wouldn't*, she told herself desperately. Not Luke. Not a man who would risk his own life to save another man. He was brave—and honourable—and everything a man ought to be. But she knew, in her heart of hearts, that she was just whistling in the dark. In reality, she didn't know Luke at all.

Only that she loved him.

CHAPTER EIGHT

THERE was a feeling of unreality about the next days. Luke telephoned Sue each evening at the guest house. To check that she was really there? That she hadn't disobeyed him?

He plied her with questions. Yes, she told him, Christopher had got off to school quite happily on Monday morning. Fred-from-the-garage had called and she had arranged with him for her own transport. He had taken the Metro in for service, so that it would be ready as soon as her driving licence came through. Fred was being very obliging. She had done a lot of shopping and filled the freezer up and she had been over to see Mary once or twice. Yes, Tony was still there but he was going abroad again soon. No, she hadn't seen any more of Vanessa. Yes, Mrs Lloyd was making her very comfortable at the guest house and there were several elderly residents staying there. She joined them in watching television in the evenings.

'Mrs Lloyd knows of a married couple who might be willing to take a job at the cottage,' she told Luke. 'The wife is experienced—she was in service at some big house before she was married. Her husband is convalescing after a bad accident on the motorway—he was a lorry driver—but he could make himself useful doing odd jobs outside. What do you think and what wages should I offer if they're willing to come?'

'Anything they ask,' Luke rapped out tersely. 'Get them, for God's sake, Sue. Let's try to get things running smoothly.'

Each time he rang she waited for him to say, 'I've

arranged about the wedding for next week, like I said,' but he didn't mention the matter, and she couldn't bring herself to ask him about it. She tried not to notice that he sounded strained and evasive when she enquired how the work was going. She reminded herself that Luke Masters was a company director—an important member of a huge corporation; that what happened to her was only one small part of his life.

On Wednesday evening he said, 'I won't ring you tomorrow, Sue, I've got a dinner booked and goodness knows what time I'll get in. Leave a message if there's anything important. I'll be seeing you on Saturday—I'll try and leave early and be in time to join you and Chris for lunch. OK?'

'I'll look forward to that,' Sue said, and tried to keep the longing out of her voice. Luke wouldn't appreciate any show of emotion from her.

'Me too,' he said. 'Goodbye, Sue dear, look after yourself.'

Sue dear! Try as she might she couldn't turn those two words into a protestation of anything more than mild affection.

On Thursday afternoon Mr and Mrs Jackson came about the job, and Sue liked them at once. Mrs Jackson was a pink-cheeked cheerful woman in her forties, with a married daughter living in Bowness; her husband tall and gaunt and quiet, showed the results of his accident in a bad limp and a long scar down one side of his face. 'But he's getting on fine now,' his wife assured Sue, 'and he'll be happy to make himself useful around the place, won't you, Eric? We've been looking for a nice living-in position since we had to sell our house when Eric was in hospital for so long.'

References were produced from the local vicar. Wages were agreed and they could move in right away; tomorrow if that was convenient. 'My daughter'll be glad of the room,' Mrs Jackson confided. 'She's expecting her third.'

Sue stood at the door and saw them off, being driven in their son-in-law's van. That was a relief, she thought, at least there would be a reliable person living here if—if—she faced the possibility grimly—if she herself found it impossible to stay. Thrusting the thought away she went upstairs to prepare a room for the Jacksons. She had to keep herself busy, to pretend that all was going to come out right in the end.

The secretary at Christopher's school telephoned later that afternoon about some special coaching in maths that Christopher was going to have. Could she speak to Mr Masters?

'I'm sorry,' Sue said. 'He's not available at present. Can I give him a message?' She wrote down the particulars.

'Could you possibly ring back tomorrow, early on?' The secretary sounded somewhat hot and bothered. 'I'm afraid there's been a bit of a muddle about it.'

Sue promised to do what she could. And that, she thought, would give her an excuse to speak to Luke this evening, however late it was. If he wasn't back from his dinner she could leave a message on his *Ansaphone* for him to ring her back. The thought of speaking to him kept her going for the rest of the afternoon.

There was a coin-operated telephone in the hall at the guest-house. Sue waited until all the residents had gone to bed before she dialled the number of Luke's flat, expecting to hear his voice on the *Ansaphone*.

But a woman's voice said, 'Yes—who is that?'

Sue said confusedly. 'Is that Mr Masters's flat? I think I must have got a wrong number——'

'My, my, the little housekeeper, isn't it?' A drawl that could belong to nobody but Vanessa. 'Something you wanted to ask Luke about? You haven't set fire to the cottage or anything, have you?' A low gurgle of laughter. 'No, my child, Luke isn't in yet—he's at some dreary dinner or other. I'm expecting him back any time now but I won't bother him unless it's something really urgent. He won't want to be faced with some stupid domestic crisis this time of the night.' Her voice dropped suggestively. 'We'll have much better things to do, if you take my meaning.'

Very slowly Sue replaced the receiver and stood staring at it, seeing nothing. She knew now that this was what she had been fearing—expecting almost—but it didn't make the pain any less.

Mrs Lloyd came out from the kitchen quarters. 'You finished 'phoning, dear? I'll put the lights out down here, then.' She drew nearer, peering into Sue's face in the dim light of the hall. 'Are you feeling all right, Miss Larkin? You don't look too good if you don't mind my saying so.'

Sue swallowed a huge, jagged lump in her throat. 'I'm fine, thanks, Mrs Lloyd. Just a bit tired, Good night.'

If she held on tightly to the banister and took one step at a time, she told herself, she might be able to get up to her room before her legs folded up under her.

Upstairs she sat on the edge of the bed, cold and sick. She couldn't stay here now, it had all been a dreadful mistake. What was she going to do? She wasn't trained for anything. Perhaps she could get a domestic job, somewhere in the Lake District but far enough from here to be sure she wouldn't have to risk bumping into Vanessa, or Chris, or—Luke. She would have to take enough money from Luke to keep her going until she got a job, but he wouldn't mind that; he'd be glad enough to be relieved of the responsibility of looking after her.

She couldn't let Auntie Meg know what a fiasco this had all been. Or Steve. Not yet, anyway. Later on, she thought bleakly, when Steve and Mariko came back to England, she would tell them what had happened, but not now. Now she was on her own. Entirely on her own, responsible for her own actions, her own mistakes.

She felt empty and dried up inside. It might help to cry but she had no tears to cry with. Sitting in the small, clean guest-house bedroom Sue faced the fact that this was all her own fault. 'You surely don't imagine you've got what it takes to hold a man like Luke, do you?' Vanessa had said contemptuously. That, Sue admitted to herself bitterly, was exactly what she *had* imagined. She had behaved like a romantic teenager pretending to be capable of handling a situation that was beyond her experience. None of it had been Luke's fault, she told herself, it had all been hers. Perhaps it was at that desolate moment that she grew up at last.

That night she didn't sleep at all. But life had to go on and in the morning she dressed and went down to have breakfast with the residents and talked about the weather just as if she were still alive, and not dead inside. Fred came as usual to drive her to the cottage and left her with a cheery wave and a, 'See you later, when I pick up young Chris at the school.'

The Jacksons arrived just before midday and were installed in their room. Mrs Jackson took immediate charge in the kitchen and consulted Sue about meals.

Sue passed a hand wearily over her forehead. It was getting increasingly difficult to make her brain work. 'There will just be Christopher and myself this evening. Mr Masters won't be home until tomorrow.'

Then she would have to tell him that she wanted to leave. She would have today as a respite, to give her

time to think out what she would say to him.
Meanwhile she would write to Auntie Meg and to
Steve and tell them how wonderful it was to be back
again near the lakes. She could talk about Chris, and
the cottage. It wouldn't be too difficult—nobody
expected her to be emotionally involved with Luke,
although Steve, she thought, might have guessed. One
day she would tell him the whole story. Luke was a
colleague and there must be no trouble between them
on her account.

She was half-way through the second letter when
she heard a car pull up outside and the front door
open. 'Sue—where are you?' Luke's voice came up the
stairs and through her open door. 'I'm home.'

She jumped up as if she'd had an electric shock.
'Here!' she tried to call but no sound came. When she
reached the top of the stairs he was standing in the hall
below, looking up, and her heart started such a crazy
tattoo that it felt as if it were going to burst. She
grabbed the rail to steady herself and after a moment
walked down the stairs putting a smile on her stiff lips.
'This *is* a surprise,' she said idiotically.

'Not too unpleasant, I hope?' It was his old ironic
tone; she hadn't heard it recently. And he was looking
strangely at her.

Mrs Jackson had heard Luke's arrival and was
hovering in the hall, looking faintly embarrassed. 'Oh,
Luke, this is Mrs Jackson,' Sue said. 'She and her
husband have just arrived.'

'Pleased to meet you, sir.' Mrs Jackson wiped her
hand on her nylon overall before she took the hand
Luke held out, saying, 'I hope you'll be very happy
here, Mrs Jackson.'

'Oh, I'm sure we will, sir. It's a lovely house and my
husband will enjoy doing the garden.' She looked at
Sue. 'There'll be one extra for supper, then, Miss

Larkin? I'll be seeing to it.' She disappeared into the kitchen.

Luke led the way into the living room. 'You've been very clever to get them, Sue,' he said. 'She seems an excellent body. I could never manage to find myself a housekeeper like that.'

Perhaps you went for the young ones, Sue thought, remembering Vanessa's spiteful words and wondering if they were true. If she could believe them it would perhaps make it easier to say what she had to say.

Luke helped himself to a drink and sank into a chair. 'I broke the record driving up,' he said. 'I wanted to be here when Chris got home this time. After last weekend's debacle,' he added. 'I was busy up to the last minute, that's why I didn't wait to 'phone. I thought I'd give you a nice surprise.' There was an edge to his tone and his smile didn't reach his eyes. 'Everything OK?' he asked.

'I think so,' Sue said. Now that he was here before her she was beginning to wonder if she could manage to get the words out that she had to say. She tried not to look too hard at him, at the dark, rugged face, the steely grey eyes that she had seen soften, the hard mouth that could look tender. It didn't mean a thing, she reminded herself. She had filled in a need in his life for a little while, that was all. She wouldn't see that special kind of tenderness again, ever.

She said, 'You got through your meetings earlier than you thought, then?'

'Yes,' he said, 'and very satisfactorily too. I want to tell you about it, you may be pleased. But first the bad news. I know I suggested that we should have the wedding next week, but I'm afraid it won't be possible. I've been in touch with the Registrar's Office and they want details of your "domicile", as they call

it, in Australia. So we'll have to postpone it for the
time being.'

This was it, then. This was the final proof. This was
what Vanessa had called Luke 'finding some excuse to
wriggle out of it'. It could hardly be plainer.

Sue sat down. Her limbs felt heavy and numb but
her voice still seemed to work. 'I think,' she said
slowly, 'that we'd better postpone it for good.'

His head jerked up. 'What the hell are you talking
about?'

She licked her dry lips. 'I've had time to think
since I've been here on my own these last few days
and I've come to the conclusion that I can't marry
you, Luke. I told you in Japan that I could never
marry without love, remember? Well—just for a
time, after we ... after ...' Her voice faltered but
now she had started she must go on. 'After we made
love you persuaded me that it would work, but it
wouldn't—not for me. We scarcely know each other.
We've both admitted that we're not in love, so what
have we got?'

His grey eyes were fixed on her, but there was no
expression at all in his face. She couldn't tell what he
was thinking. 'I'd have thought it was obvious what
we've got,' he said.

'You mean—sex?' It was extraordinary, now that
she had started, how easy it was to talk to him. She
wouldn't have believed it. 'Yes, I admit that I enjoyed
your lovemaking. I'm sure you're an expert—although
I've nothing to compare it with, as you know.' She
was actually able to produce a small smile. 'But that's
not enough to found a marriage on—not even a
marriage of convenience, as this would be.'

There was a long, horrible silence. Then, 'I see,' he
said tightly. 'At least I think I do. As you seem to have
thought it out very thoroughly how do you propose

that we should go on from here? Do you want to leave?'

His face was blank, shuttered. Well, of course I do, she almost screamed. You don't think I'd stay to see you here with Vanessa, do you? But she said calmly, 'I thought I'd try to get a job. I don't want to leave the Lakes now that I've got back here.'

He nodded. 'As you like.' He looked deadly tired now and Sue had a quick moment of remorse that she had unloaded this on him at the end of what must have been a stressful business week. 'But leave it over the weekend, will you? Let Chris get used to the idea of Mrs Jackson first. There have been so many changes for the poor kid—he's had a bad time these last months.'

'But—but he'll be all right now he's getting his mother back, surely?' The words seemed to come out of their own accord. Sue hadn't planned to say them and now that they were said she was appalled.

Appalled by the look on his face too. All through this horrible little scene he had looked his usual controlled self but now he jumped up, glaring down at her, his eyes like steel rapiers. 'What the hell are you talking about?' he shouted. 'Whatever gave you that idea?' Both his hands were gripping the arms of her chair as he leaned over her.

She shrank back as if he had actually struck her. 'I—I thought . . .'

'Well, you shouldn't bloody well think,' he roared.

'I thought you were still in love with her—with Vanessa. Everything—*everything* pointed to it.'

He pulled her out of the chair and took her by the shoulders. 'How can I be in love with that bitch? I'm in love with you, you stupid girl.' He shook her until her teeth rattled. 'Don't you *know*—couldn't you *see* that I've been waiting for you to come round to the idea that you might love me?' he shouted. 'And now I suppose what you're trying to tell me is that you've fallen for that brother of Mary's—Tony, or whatever his bloody name is. What a God-awful mess!'

'No, no, I haven't,' Sue yelled back at him. 'I'm not in love with Tony. I'm in love with you, I have been all the time.' She flung her arms round him. 'I'm absolutely crazy about you. When I thought you were going back to Vanessa I nearly threw myself in the lake.'

Then they were clinging together, kissing wildly, recklessly, until Sue was gasping for breath. 'Let's go upstairs,' muttered Luke.

It was at that moment that the telephone rang across the room.

Luke took his mouth from Sue's long enough to say, 'Let it ring,' but Sue had already gone to answer it. After a moment she turned back to Luke. 'It's the school secretary,' she said, her face pale. 'She says they're a little worried because Chris's mother came to the school this morning to take Chris out to lunch. She promised to bring him back by two o'clock at the latest because he's booked for a private maths coaching session but they haven't returned yet and——'

Luke grabbed the 'phone from her and spoke into it rapidly. 'Masters here—no, they haven't come back here. Yes, I'm sorry about that. Leave it with me, will you? I'll be in touch.'

He replaced the receiver, his face grim. 'I've been afraid of something like this happening.' He ran a hand distractedly through his hair. 'Since last night I guessed she'd try to take it out on me.' He turned a haggard face to Sue. 'I'll give it an hour and if there's no news I'll contact the police.' He went across to the window and peered out. It wouldn't get dark just yet, but already a mist was coming down over the lake and the trees were dripping dolefully.

Sue joined him and pressed her head against his shoulder. 'Oh, Luke, I'm so sorry.' What else was there to say? He drew her against him and held her tightly as if he found comfort in her closeness and they stayed like that, not speaking. Sue found herself praying, Let Chris come back, please let him come back.

She remembered the way he had gone off on Monday morning. 'Do you think I'll be able to have one more ride on Flossie before they take her away?' he had pleaded. 'Tony's leaving tomorrow—will they take the horses away then? Will you ask Auntie Mary to keep them for just one more week?'

'I'll try,' she had promised as she waved him goodbye and he had called back, 'Thanks, Sue, you're a trump.'

That had warmed her heart, but now she felt like weeping for Christopher, and for Luke, both of them trapped in one of these horrid tug-of-love situations. But did Vanessa really love her son? Sue doubted it, she doubted it very much.

Almost, her fear managed to eclipse the joy that was bubbling up inside her. Almost, but not quite. Standing by the window, with Luke's arm holding her close, she buried her head against his shoulder and tasted the salt of tears on her lips as she tried to take in the incredible fact that he loved her.

Suddenly he was alert. 'Thank God, here they are,' he muttered, and Sue heard the swish of tyres on the gravel of the drive. Luke made for the front door and she followed behind him to see Vanessa get out of the car. Vanessa—alone.

'Where is he? What have you done with him?' Luke's voice was low and infinitely dangerous.

Vanessa strolled past him into the drawing room, her pale fur coat slung round her shoulders, her mouth petulant. 'Hasn't he turned up yet—I thought he'd probably hitched a lift back here.' She sank into a chair. 'God—I'm worn out, I've been driving all over the county trying to find that idiot boy.' She turned her slanting green eyes on Luke. 'Get me a drink, there's a love.'

He ignored that. He went and stood over her and Sue winced at the controlled menace in his voice as he said, 'Tell me—now, this minute—what you've done with him or I'll have the police here and put you on a charge.'

Vanessa's laugh rang very false. '*Darling*, I've told you. I haven't done anything with him. I left him in the car while we stopped for a drink and when we came out he'd gone. He'd been awkward all the time—kept on moaning about some horse or other that was going to be taken away. Wanted me to drive him back here.'

'You stopped for a drink—where?'

Vanessa yawned. 'Sweetie, *I* don't know where. Somewhere the other side of Lancaster, I think. Chris was throwing a tantrum and I thought I'd leave him on his own to get over it. Don't look at me like that, Luke. He'll find his way back, he's not a toddler any longer.'

Sue put a hand on Luke's arm. 'I wonder—something I've just thought of——' She went over the telephone and dialled Mary's number.

Mary answered herself. 'Hullo, Sue, I was just going to ring you.'

'Listen, Mary,' Sue broke in anxiously. 'Have you seen anything of Chris this afternoon? He's missing and I just wondered——'

'That was what I was going to ring you about—to

ask if he was home yet. Old Joe has just been in to tell me that he came over from his cottage to take a look at the horses and he finds that Flossie has gone.'

Sue's fingers closed round the receiver in a painful grip. 'Gone—when? Does he know? Can Chris saddle her up himself?'

'Yes, after a fashion—he's been learning, but——'

'We're coming over,' Sue said and slammed down the 'phone.

Luke's head was close to hers. 'You heard that?' she said and he nodded. 'Get a coat,' he rapped out and without a glance at Vanessa he strode to the door.

It took only a few minutes to drive to the farm. Mary was waiting for them in the stables, her face anxious, Joe, the ancient farm-worker, hovering in the background. 'Peter's gone to a sale in Kendal, and Tony left yesterday. There's no sign of Flossie.' She bit her lip. 'And Chris being missing—it's too much of a coincidence, don't you think?'

Luke looked at Sue and then up at the sky. He said, 'There's almost an hour of light left. May we take two of the horses, Mary?'

The urgency in his voice reached both the girls and Mary said, 'Of course. You can ride Bounty, Luke, and Sue can have Rosie. I wish I could come with you but my doctor's put his foot down about riding and Peter would never forgive me if anything happened to the infant.'

Luke said, 'Are you game, Sue?' He didn't have to ask. She was already reaching up for Rosie's saddle.

Mary watched them go. 'I'll tell Peter when he comes in,' she said. 'He may be able to think of something. Good luck,' she added, her voice unsteady.

Luke kept his horse close to Sue's until they reached a place where the paths divided. He reined in and said, 'Have you any idea which way he might go?'

'It's just a chance,' she said. 'But when we were out at the weekend with Tony we rode over towards Ambleside. There's a hut beside the stream, where we stopped for a picnic. He might just have remembered and made for that.'

'OK, you go that way and I'll tackle the higher paths. If it begins to get dark turn back immediately—promise? You think you can find the way?'

Sue said quietly, 'I know every yard of these fells, I won't get lost. We'll find him, Luke, I'm sure we will.'

He sat very still for a moment, looking at her intently, and Sue's heart turned over with love and compassion as she saw the lines of anxiety etching deep grooves round his mouth. Then, 'Bless you, darling,' he said raggedly and a moment later he and his mount had gone, climbing up into the vague, shifting mist that was beginning to fall over the fells.

Sue rode on quite slowly. It was cold but she felt no cold. Inside her the knowledge that Luke loved her was glowing like a slow-burning fire, spreading through her body, warming every little bit of her, even allaying her anxiety about Chris, and she hugged the incredible fact to herself as she went.

Rosie, the amiable chestnut mare, picked her way along the rough track and Sue had to do little more than sit and hold the reins. As she went she called out constantly: 'Chris—Chris—are you there—Chris . . .' Her own voice echoed back to her out of the emptiness. Time crept by, infinitely extended by the strangeness, the loneliness of the fells at a time like this. Searching—searching . . . was this how Daddy had searched that night four years ago? Knowing that human lives depended on his colleagues and him? That somewhere up here the cold was creeping into exhausted limbs that could struggle no further?

But that night had been different, she told herself

quickly. Chris, if he was here—and now she had little doubt that he was here somewhere—wouldn't be in any immediate danger from cold. It was chilly, certainly, but that other night there had been thick snow on the fells and an icy wind blowing. This time there was only the mist—and the darkness falling. 'If it begins to get dark turn back immediately—promise.' Luke had said.

But she hadn't promised and she was going to reach that hut, darkness or not. Rosie wasn't too happy now, she was probably wondering why she was out here instead of in her warm stall with a bucketful of oats. Sue urged her on but a few minutes later she planted her four feet down and that was that.

Sue slipped from the saddle and pulled the reins over the mare's head. 'All right, pal, we'll soldier on together, shall we?' She patted the warm nose and talked gently as she persuaded Rosie to be led onward along the track. 'We've got to go on, old girl, we've got to reach that hut, because Chris is there, I know he is.'

The mist was getting thicker all the time, it was a grey swirl now, in her mouth, catching her throat as she went on calling. When the sound of her own voice died away the silence was eerie. But she *knew* he was there. It was very strange how she knew but she did. In her mind she could see the hut where they had had their picnic. She could see every bit of it—the wooden veranda outside, the rustic poles that formed the railings, the long benches inside to offer rest to the tourists who walked the fells in the summer.

Chris *had* to be there. Inside Sue was such an upsurge of the sheer joy of knowing herself loved that it filled every bit of her and overflowed into a certainty of finding Chris, because she was finding him for Luke. She didn't think of it like that, in fact she wasn't thinking at all, she was just stumbling on, leading the reluctant Rosie, calling every few minutes, her eyes searching for the outline of the hut, which, she was sure, must appear any moment. It must be more than half an hour since she had parted with Luke and it was almost dark now. Only a kind of sixth sense kept her on the track.

'Chris—Chris—are you there?' From somewhere ahead of her there was a faint reply, she was sure of it. She broke into a stumbling run, urging the mare behind her. 'Come on, Rosie, come on, girl.' She was almost sobbing in her eagerness.

There was just enough light left to see the outline of the hut. She stepped up on to the wooden platform, tying Rosie clumsily to the upright. 'Chris, are you there?'

'I'm here,' came a very small voice from the inside of the hut and Sue ran blindly across the floor and took the small boy in her arms.

'Are you all right, Chris? Are you hurt?'

He was crying now. 'I d-don't think so. I was just going to start to walk back. Sue, it's you, isn't it—I can't see you.' He clung to her.

'Are you hurt?' she said again, and felt him shake his head. 'No—but—but I've lost Flossie. That's the awful thing. The g-girth slipped and I fell off and—and when I got up I couldn't find her. Oh Sue, what if she doesn't come back? What if someone steals her?'

'Don't worry Chris, she'll find her own way home, I'm sure of it. She'll probably be there by the time we get back.'

The boy shivered. 'How *can* we get back? It's miles and miles and it's dark as anything.'

'We'll manage,' Sue said with more conviction than she felt. 'I've got Rosie tied up outside. You can ride home and I'll lead her. I just wish we had a torch.'

'I've got a torch in my pocket, I'd forgotten.' Chris fumbled in the dark. 'Here you are.'

Sue laughed. 'You must be a boy scout,' she said. 'We can flash it around as we go and perhaps Daddy will see it. He's out here somewhere—we've both been looking for you.'

Chris drew a little nearer. 'Will he be cross with me?' he said in a very small voice. 'I ran away from Mummy.'

'Oh, I shouldn't think so,' Sue said practically. 'Come on, let's go. Here, put my jacket on—I won't need it, I'll be walking.'

Outside she heaved Chris up into the saddle of the big mare. In the torchlight he looked very small and frightened sitting up there.

'OK, Chris?'

He answered sturdily, 'I'm fine.'

The pace was faster on the return journey. Rosie undoubtedly knew that she was on her way home and now and again she broke into a slow trot, so that Sue had to run to keep up. She hadn't much breath left but she urged Chris to go on calling, and the cry of 'Daddy—Daddy . . .' echoed across the fells. Sue calculated that they must be within half a mile of the farm when she heard Luke's voice calling. 'Here,' she yelled back. 'We're here,' and the form of the big black horse and the man leading him appeared like a miracle through the mist.

Luke wasted no time in talking. Once he had assured himself that neither Chris nor Sue was hurt he took firm charge. 'You get up on Bounty, Sue, and I'll lead both horses in.' His arm was round her to help her into the saddle. 'Why haven't you got a coat on? You'll be frozen.' He turned the torch on Chris, wearing Sue's jacket, the sleeves dangling over his hands. 'Oh—I see. Well, we'll do a swap all round.

You wear mine,' and Sue was pushed, none too gently, into Luke's own jacket. Her teeth were chattering now, from reaction as much as cold, and she clutched the jacket round her, revelling in the warmth that came from Luke's body.

'We must look like a camel-train,' she shouted, as they set out along the track again, Luke leading Rosie, with Chris mounted, and Sue following behind on the big black horse, Bounty, her dangling feet not reaching the stirrups. She was beginning to feel an extraordinary light-headed euphoria. It was all coming right. Everything was coming right in this wonderful, wonderful world.

Peter and Mary were both waiting for them as they clumped through the gate into the farm-yard. Mary was weeping with relief and wiping away her tears, laughing, 'Don't mind me—it's just my interesting condition. I get worked up about things.'

Peter was a practical man, a man of few words. 'You get these two home and into hot baths, Luke,' he said, opening the door of Luke's car and bundling Sue and Chris inside. 'I'll see to the horses. By the way, Flossie came trotting home half an hour ago, as bright as a button.' Sue felt Chris's body relax against her in the back of the car. 'Good show,' he muttered sleepily.

'See you all tomorrow,' Mary called out as Luke got into the driving seat, and he called back, 'You bet. We'll thank you properly then.'

Mrs Jackson was hovering in the hall when they got home. She looked at Luke and said rather uncertainly, 'The lady that was here left soon after you and Miss Larkin went out, sir. I asked her if she would like to leave a message but she——'

Luke interrupted with a brief, 'That's quite all right Mrs Jackson. Now, we'd better look after these two, hadn't we? They've been wandering out on the fells, which is a very foolish thing to do this time of the day, isn't it, Chris?'

Chris looked up at his father's face and away again quickly. 'Yes,' he mumbled. 'I'm sorry, Dad.'

His father put a hand on his shoulder. 'I wasn't going to bawl you out, Chris,' he said quietly. 'You go with Mrs Jackson and she'll get you a hot drink, won't you, Mrs Jackson?'

Mrs Jackson was a Lakelander herself. One glance at Chris, peaky and shivering, and she took him in charge. 'You come along with me, young man, a nice cup of cocoa is what you need first of all.' She looked towards Sue. 'The water's lovely and hot, Miss Larkin. If you'd like a hot bath first, then I've got some supper on for you afterwards.'

Chris went along willingly, no doubt glad to be spared the possibility of having to make explanations to his father.

Luke turned to Sue, his mouth twisting bitterly. 'So—Vanessa couldn't even wait to find out if Chris was safe.'

He sighed as if he were casting a heavy burden from his back, then he nodded to Sue and said, 'Go along and have your bath, my darling, but don't lock the door, I'll bring you up a reviver.' Sue, who was beginning to feel very shivery by now, made for the bathroom and was soon immersed in gloriously hot water. A minute or two later there was a tap on the door and Luke appeared, a steaming beaker in his hand, grinning widely.

'What a beautiful sight!' He came over to the side of the bath as Sue wriggled down to try to cover herself completely. 'Drink this up.'

One pink arm appeared from beneath the water and Sue clutched the beaker and lifted herself to sip the hot toddy, while Luke stood and watched her.

'Go away,' she giggled. She was feeling decidedly lightheaded at the moment and the toddy tasted very strongly of something alcoholic.

Luke ignored her request. Instead he pulled up the bathroom stool and sat down. 'I haven't thanked you for what you did for Chris. I said you were a star, Sue darling. I should have said super-star. I love you more than I can tell you.' He picked up a fat pink sponge and squeezed it over her shoulders and her pretty pointed breasts as she sat up to drink the toddy.

'Do you really love me, Luke?' Sue said dreamily. 'I can't believe it yet.'

He dropped the sponge and his hand slowly traced the shape of her, under the water, making her shiver deliciously. 'I'd like to show you how much here and now, but I'll try to contain myself a little longer. In the spring, when the cherry blossom is out, we'll go back to Japan and stay on a beautiful island I know, in a real Japanese inn where each room has a communal bath.' He laughed softly. 'That idea has distinct possibilities.'

He got to his feet. 'Now, hurry up and come down, I've got some news for you.' He leaned over and kissed her mouth and her wet cheeks and the tips of her breasts lingeringly, and then, with a long regretful sigh, and a wicked grin, he left her.

CHAPTER NINE

'I THINK,' said Sue dreamily, 'that I shall wake up soon in my little room in Langeroo and find I've been imagining all this.'

It was hours later. Christopher had gone to bed, blissfully happy because he had managed to extract a promise from Sue that, if Mary agreed, she would exercise Rosie and Flossie so that they needn't be sent away for the winter, and that they would ride together in the school holidays.

Now Sue, wrapped in a fleecy camel dressing-gown of Luke's after her bath, and replete with a tasty supper which the excellent Mrs Jackson had somehow managed to conjure up out of the freezer, was curled up against Luke on the sofa in the living room. The long velvet curtains were pulled together against the chill and mist outside, the lights were dimmed to one shaded standard lamp, apple-logs burnt fragrantly on the fire.

'I mean,' she went on seriously, 'that it's too perfect to be true. Me being here in Lakeland in this beautiful house and the most wonderful, handsome, intelligent, man in the world saying he loves me. It's just like one of my books—the nicer kind.'

Luke went through a ridiculous pantomime of preening himself.

'Now that's what I like to hear,' he chuckled. 'It's not imagination, my darling, it's all quite true except, I fear, the intelligent part. I've been thinking lately that I'm the world's biggest mug.' He lifted her hair and kissed her neck lingeringly. 'But I know what you mean. I'd begun to believe myself that happiness like this wasn't possible.'

Sue asked the age-old question. 'When did you first know?'

'That I loved you?' He stared into the fire, considering. 'I think perhaps when I wakened up that morning in Tokyo and found you in my bed. You looked so young and sweet and—and untouched.'

'But you were absolutely beastly to me.'

He drew her even closer, as if to reassure himself that she was really there. 'That was my defence mechanism. You see, after Vanessa I vowed I wasn't ever going to risk committing myself again. I'd been infatuated with her for ten years, she was a virus in my blood. I knew what she was like—entirely selfish, ruthless, demanding—but somehow I couldn't get rid of the virus. It seemed to me that while I was still in danger I couldn't let myself fall in love again. But of course, I did, only I wouldn't admit it to myself,' he added ruefully. 'I think I finally knew what was happening to me when we went to that lake in Kyoto. That was when I asked you to come back with me. I just knew that I couldn't let you go out of my life.'

Sue nodded slowly. 'You said once that love is a sickness,' she said slowly. 'Do you still think that?'

'Not the kind of love I feel for you,' he told her, pressing his cheek against her hair, damp still from her bath. 'I adore you, I worship you, my lovely, warm, generous girl. The love I feel for you could never be a sickness, only a cure. When Vanessa turned up at my flat in London the other night I was scared—at first. I thought, "Great heaven, now it's all going to start again." I was even afraid I might be going to be swine enough to let you down. You can't think to what depths I sunk. Then she began to put on her great seduction act, just like she always had done before.

And suddenly—it was like lightning striking—it didn't mean a blind thing to me. All I could think of was you, up here with Chris, waiting for me. All I wanted was to get back to you. I could have danced round the flat, singing like a lunatic. Instead of which I showed her the door and told her in no uncertain manner that there was nothing doing, that you and I were going to be married as soon as it could be arranged.'

His mouth tightened as he stared into the fire. 'There was a most unpleasant scene, but eventually I got rid of her, and after that I sat down and poured myself a stiff drink and thought, "I'm free. My God, I'm free at last." You can't imagine how wonderful it felt. I couldn't wait to get back to you. If I hadn't had this important meeting next morning I'd have jumped into the car and started then and there.'

Sue snuggled closer to him, understanding so much that she hadn't understood before, loving him more than ever for being honest with her.

After a time she said, 'All those perfumes and things in the bathroom cupboard—were those Vanessa's?'

He jerked his head round. 'Yes—why?'

'She told me that you wouldn't marry me—that you made a habit of engaging girls as housekeepers and promising to marry them and then wriggling out of it when you got tired of them. She told me that was what would happen in my case. And—and then I saw the photograph of her on your desk—and Mary told me how devoted you were to her—and—and you had made it quite plain that you didn't love me. And then when you said that the Registrar had told you that the wedding would have to be postponed I thought you were just breaking it gently.'

He shook his head. 'Not so, it was the literal truth.' He leaned forward, burying his face in his hands. After a moment he looked up at her in the firelight.

'Vanessa was always an accomplished liar. She probably heard gossip from that Cynthia woman in Ambleside she was so thick with that I'd had a succession of housekeepers and she must have invented the rest. Although I must admit one or two of them had certain—er—aspirations, which filled me with alarm. So that was why you greeted me with the news that you were walking out on me? You thought I was the Lakeland Bluebeard?'

Sue laughed unsteadily. 'Not really. I just didn't see how you could—how I could satisfy you—after *her*. I was green with jealousy of her—she looked so—so devastatingly lovely.'

Luke groaned. 'Some poisonous snakes are devastatingly lovely too. My poor darling, I should never have let you in for a concentrated dose of Vanessa. She's lethal. Yes, those perfumes and things were hers. If you'd seen the succession of housekeepers you wouldn't have been misled. They weren't exactly the type to use French perfume. I should have chucked the stuff out months ago but I couldn't bring myself to do it. I suppose it wasn't until she suggested that we should get together again that I really knew I was cured of the sickness, that I could never want her back in my life again.'

His hands caressed Sue's cheek, her neck, gently. 'After all this soul-searching I suggest that we consign Vanessa's memory to the remote past. I don't think she'll try anything on again.'

'Do you think that she really meant to kidnap Chris?' Sue asked.

'God knows,' he said. 'It's something I've always been scared of—that she'd try to get back at me through Chris. I never knew what tricks she'd get up to. That was why I came dashing up here the first time she put in an appearance. I'm not altogether sure

what happened this afternoon, but I gather that one of
Vanessa's boy-friends was in the car and that's what
alarmed him. That and the fact that she had promised
to take him back to school and it became plain that she
had no such intention. It was pretty spunky of him to
escape.'

Sue said, her mouth soft, 'He's a pretty spunky little
boy. Did you find out how he managed to get back
here?'

'He didn't say very much. Apparently he got a lift in
a lorry as far as Windermere and walked the three
miles from there. He was desperate to get back to
Flossie before she was taken away.'

They were silent for a time, close together with the
closeness of lovers—and friends. After a while Sue felt
in the capacious pocket of Luke's dressing gown and
brought out a small parcel. 'This is for you,' she said
rather shyly. 'I got hooked on the Japanese habit of
giving presents.' As he tore off the wrapping she went
on, 'I meant to put a card in with a corny message
saying "Ships that pass in the night". I thought
perhaps you might come across it some time and
remember the girl you met in Japan.'

He held the tiny perfect model ship in his hand in
silence and she saw a muscle working in his cheek.
Then he laughed rather unsteadily. 'I think I'm going
to burst into tears. Thank you, my darling, it's an
exquisite thing and I'll treasure it always.' He bent his
head and kissed her very tenderly.

'And now,' he said. 'I have something for you too.
This is beginning to feel like Christmas.' He drew
out a ring-box from his pocket and opened it to
disclose a single-stone sapphire set in a narrow band
of gold. He slipped it on her finger and it glittered
like blue fire in the lamp-light. He pressed his lips
against her hand. 'Yes. The colour of your eyes, and

a good guess for size,' he said contentedly. 'Do you like it?'

Sue gazed down at her hand. 'Now *I'm* going to burst into tears,' she said. She threw her arms round Luke's neck and hugged him wildly. 'It's the most beautiful ring in the world and I'm the luckiest girl,' she sobbed. 'Oh darling, I do love you so very very much.'

It was some considerable time before either of them spoke again. Then Sue sat up and tried to pull the dressing-gown straight around her.

'We must be sensible,' she said with mock modesty. 'What was it you were going to tell me? You said . . .'

He sat up abruptly, scattering cushions. 'Lord, yes. You put everything else out of my head, you witch you.' He kissed the tip of her nose. 'It's great news—at least I hope you'll think so too. These meetings we've been having—I didn't tell you before in case it didn't come off—but now it's pretty certain that we'll be taking over a big textile mill only about forty miles from here and we're going to develop it even further. Put in a new polyester plant among other things. I'm going to be in charge of the project . . . So I'll be able to commute each day and you won't have to be a weekend wife, my lovely. How about that? And probably there'll be a job for Steve there too, so he won't be so far away.'

Sue's eyes were full of tears. 'Now I *know* I'm dreaming.'

His hand, warm and tender, found its way under the dressing gown and closed over her breast and tremors of longing began to shake her body. Somewhere a clock struck midnight and Luke got to his feet. 'I can think of one sure way to convince you that you're awake. Come on up, my love, it'll be cosy in bed.'

'I've moved all my things out . . .' she began.

'Well, you can move them in again.'

'Mr and Mrs Jackson . . .' she protested weakly.

His chuckle was deep and low in his throat. 'I'm not asking Mrs J. to sleep with me, my funny darling, I'm asking you. We're going to be married in a few days and I'm aching for you—you, and not another woman in the world. Don't hold out on me, Sue. Please, sweetheart.'

She felt him tremble against her as they went up the stairs together and as they reached the bedroom and sank on to the big bed her arms went up round his neck and her mouth lifted to his in a surge of longing.

'I never managed to hold out on you, did I?' she whispered. 'So it wouldn't be much good beginning now, would it?'

WORLDWIDE LIBRARY IS YOUR TICKET TO ROMANCE, ADVENTURE AND EXCITEMENT

Experience it all in these big, bold Bestsellers— Yours exclusively from WORLDWIDE LIBRARY WHILE QUANTITIES LAST

To receive these Bestsellers, complete the order form, detach and send together with your check or money order (include 75¢ postage and handling), payable to WORLDWIDE LIBRARY, to:

In the U.S.
WORLDWIDE LIBRARY
Box 52040
Phoenix, AZ
85072-2040

In Canada
WORLDWIDE LIBRARY
P.O. Box 2800, 5170 Yonge Street
Postal Station A, Willowdale, Ontario
M2N 6J3

Quant.	Title	Price
_____	**WILD CONCERTO**, Anne Mather	$2.95
_____	**A VIOLATION**, Charlotte Lamb	$3.50
_____	**SECRETS**, Sheila Holland	$3.50
_____	**SWEET MEMORIES**, LaVyrle Spencer	$3.50
_____	**FLORA**, Anne Weale	$3.50
_____	**SUMMER'S AWAKENING**, Anne Weale	$3.50
_____	**FINGER PRINTS**, Barbara Delinsky	$3.50
	DREAMWEAVER,	
_____	Felicia Gallant/Rebecca Flanders	$3.50
_____	**EYE OF THE STORM**, Maura Seger	$3.50
_____	**HIDDEN IN THE FLAME**, Anne Mather	$3.50
_____	**ECHO OF THUNDER**, Maura Seger	$3.95
_____	**DREAM OF DARKNESS**, Jocelyn Haley	$3.95
_____		

	YOUR ORDER TOTAL	$_____
	New York and Arizona residents add appropriate sales tax	$_____
	Postage and Handling	$ .75
	I enclose	$_____

NAME _____

ADDRESS _____ APT.# _____

CITY _____

STATE/PROV. _____ ZIP/POSTAL CODE _____

WW3

Coming Next Month in Harlequin Romances!

2749   A MATTER OF MARNIE   Rosemary Badger
Convincing an Australian construction tycoon that his
grandmother has been neglected is a formidable task. Living with
him in order to care for the woman is an even greater challenge.

2750   THE PERFECT CHOICE   Melissa Forsythe
A voice student in Vienna seldom turns men's heads. So when a
handsome stranger woos her, she's in too deep by the time she
discovers his motive for choosing her over her beautiful friend.

2751   SAFE HARBOUR   Rosalie Henaghan
This trustworthy secretary weathers her boss's changeable moods
until his woman friend predicts an end to Anna's working days—
and sets out to make her prophecy come true.

2752   NEVER THE TIME AND THE PLACE   Betty Neels
The consulting surgeon at a London hospital disturbs his ward sister's
natural serenity. She's having enough trouble coping with a broken
engagement without having to put up with his arrogance.

2753   A WILL TO LOVE   Edwina Shore
That the family's Queensland homestead should be sold is
unthinkable. But the only way to save it—according to her
grandfather's will—is to marry the same man who rejected her
four years ago.

2754   HE WAS THE STRANGER   Sheila Strutt
The manager of Milk River Ranch knew that a male relative would
inherit her uncle's spread. But why did the beneficiary have to be a
writer who would either sell out or take over completely?

What readers say about Harlequin romance fiction...

"I absolutely adore Harlequin romances! They are fun and relaxing to read, and each book provides a wonderful escape."
—N.E.,* Pacific Palisades, California

"Harlequin is the best in romantic reading."
—K.G.,* Philadelphia, Pennsylvania

"Harlequins have been my passport to the world. I have been many places without ever leaving my doorstep."
—P.Z.,* Belvedere, Illinois

"My praise for the warmth and adventure your books bring into my life."
—D.F.,* Hicksville, New York

"A pleasant way to relax after a busy day."
—P.W.,* Rector, Arkansas

*Names available on request.

PASSIONATE!
CAPTIVATING!
SOPHISTICATED!

Harlequin Presents...

**The favorite fiction
of women the world over!**

Beautiful contemporary romances that
touch every emotion of a woman's heart—
passion and joy, jealousy and heartache...
but most of all...love.

Fascinating settings in the exotic
reaches of the world—
from the bustle of an international capital
to the paradise of a tropical island.

**All this and much, much more
in the pages of**

Harlequin Presents...

Wherever paperback books are sold, or through
Harlequin Reader Service

In the U.S.
2504 West Southern Avenue
Tempe, AZ 85282

In Canada
P.O. Box 2800, Postal Station A
5170 Yonge Street
Willowdale, Ontario M2N 6J3

**No one touches the heart of a woman
quite like Harlequin!**

P-111

Can you keep a secret?

You can keep this one plus 4 free novels

FREE BOOKS/GIFT COUPON

Mail to   **Harlequin Reader Service**®

In the U.S.
2504 West Southern Ave.
Tempe, AZ 85282

In Canada
P.O. Box 2800, Station "A"
5170 Yonge Street
Willowdale, Ontario M2N 6J3

YES! Please send me 4 free Harlequin Romance® novels and my free surprise gift. Then send me 6 brand-new novels every month as they come off the presses. Bill me at the low price of $1.65 each ($1.75 in Canada)—a 11% saving off the retail price. There are no shipping, handling or other hidden costs. There is no minimum number of books I must purchase. I can always return a shipment and cancel at any time. Even if I never buy another book from Harlequin, the 4 free novels and the surprise gift are mine to keep forever.

_____
Name   (PLEASE PRINT)

_____
Address   Apt. No.

_____
City   State/Prov.   Zip/Postal Code

This offer is limited to one order per household and not valid to present subscribers. Price is subject to change.

MSR–SUB–1

Just what the woman on the go needs!

BOOKMATE

The perfect "mate" for all Harlequin paperbacks!

Holds paperbacks open for hands-free reading!

- **TRAVELING**
- **VACATIONING**
- **AT WORK** • **IN BED**
- **COOKING** • **EATING**
- **STUDYING**

Perfect size for all standard paperbacks, this wonderful invention makes reading a pure pleasure! Ingenious design holds paperback books OPEN and FLAT so even wind can't ruffle pages—leaves your hands free to do other things. Reinforced, wipe-clean vinyl-covered holder flexes to let you turn pages without undoing the strap...supports paperbacks so well, they have the strength of hardcovers!

Snaps closed for easy carrying.

Available now. Send your name, address, and zip or postal code, along with a check or money order for just $4.99 + .75¢ for postage & handling (for a total of $5.74) payable to Harlequin Reader Service for to:

Harlequin Reader Service

In the U.S.A.
2504 West Southern Ave.
Tempe, AZ 85282

In Canada
P.O. Box 2800, Postal Station A
5170 Yonge Street,
Willowdale, Ont. M2N 5T5

MATE-1R